What Others Are Saying
about R.J. Patterson

"R.J. Patterson does a fantastic job at keeping you engaged and interested. I look forward to more from this talented author."

- Aaron Patterson
bestselling author of SWEET DREAMS

DEAD SHOT

"Small town life in southern Idaho might seem quaint and idyllic to some. But when local newspaper reporter Cal Murphy begins to uncover a series of strange deaths that are linked to a sticky spider web of deception, the lid on the peaceful town is blown wide open. Told with all the energy and bravado of an old pro, first-timer R.J. Patterson hits one out of the park his first time at bat with *Dead Shot*. It's that good."

- Vincent Zandri
bestselling author of THE REMAINS

"You can tell R.J. knows what it's like to live in the newspaper world, but with *Dead Shot*, he's proven that he also can write one heck of a murder mystery."

- Josh Katzowitz
NFL writer for CBSSports.com
& author of Sid Gillman: Father of the Passing Game

"Patterson has a mean streak about a mile wide and puts his two main characters through quite a horrible ride, which makes for good reading."

- Richard D., reader

DEAD LINE

"This book kept me on the edge of m
really want to put it down. R.J. Patt
back for more."

3-time .
and play-by-play .

"Like a John Grisham novel, from the very start I was pulled right into the story and couldn't put the book down. It was as if I personally knew and cared about what happened to each of the main characters. Every chapter ended with so much excitement and suspense I had to continue to read until I learned how it ended, even though it kept me up until 3:00 A.M.

- Ray F., reader

DEAD IN THE WATER

"In Dead in the Water, R.J. Patterson accurately captures the action-packed saga of a what could be a real-life college football scandal. The sordid details will leave readers flipping through the pages as fast as a hurry-up offense."

- Mark Schlabach,
ESPN college sports columnist and
co-author of *Called to Coach*
and *Heisman: The Man Behind the Trophy*

THE WARREN OMISSIONS

"What can be more fascinating than a super high concept novel that reopens the conspiracy behind the JFK assassination while the threat of a global world war rests in the balance? With his new novel, *The Warren Omissions*, former journalist turned bestselling author R.J. Patterson proves he just might be the next worthy successor to Vince Flynn."

- Vincent Zandri
bestselling author of THE REMAINS

BEHIND ENEMY LINES

A Titus Black novel

R.J. PATTERSON

BEHIND ENEMY LINES
© Copyright 2019 R.J. Patterson

First Print Edition 2020

Cover Design by Books Covered

Published in the United States of America
Green E-Books
Boise Idaho 83713

For Scott Rigsby, for his friendship
and inspiring thousands to do more
than they ever dreamed possible

CHAPTER 1

August 6
USS Illinois
Sea of Okhotsk, off coast
of Kamchatka Peninsula

TITUS BLACK CHECKED all his scuba gear one final time as the lockout trunk filled up with water. He took a deep breath to calm his nerves. Missions that involved time in the ocean ranked last in his list of favorite assignments.

"How are you doing in there?" asked Christina Shields, Black's handler at the secret black ops program Firestorm, in her sultry voice.

"It's a day at the beach," Black said.

"For most people, that'd be a good thing," she said. "But I know you're not like most people."

"Give me a mountain with five hostiles on the ridge any day."

"That'll be waiting for you once you get out of the water."

Black tightened his mask again. "It's the only thing that's saving this operation for me."

"Well, save my afternoon by making this quick because I've got plans later today."

"So is it a hot date, or are you heading to the shooting range again?"

"It's a day that ends in the letter *y*, isn't it?"

Black chuckled. "Maybe someday I'll go with you and show you how to hit the bullseye."

"You former spooks are all alike," she said. "You think that because during training you spent a few hours emptying magazines at a target that you can outshoot me."

"So, it's a date?"

"You wish," she said with a sneer. "Isn't that trunk filled up yet?"

The water had reached Black's shoulders, and it was almost time to launch out of the sub and into the water.

"I'm going dark, but stay tuned in case I need you." He took a deep breath and put the regulator in his mouth.

A minute later, the hatch opened, allowing Black to swim up to the tower and open the Special Forces box. He removed all the supplies he needed, including the propulsion device that would help him slice through Okhotsk's swift currents. He tapped on the side of the sub before pushing off with his legs and heading in the direction of shore.

Without any moonlight to assist him, Black relied on his headlamp as he navigated through the dark waters. He hummed along, keeping an eye out for anything approaching. After a few minutes, he happened upon a school of fish that encircled him and matched his speed until they all made a sharp turn right, clearing the way for him.

After a few minutes, he checked his depth gauge and noticed he was venturing into shallower water. He slowed down and let his feet touch on the rocky bottom. With his eyes just above the surface, Black saw the faint outline of the craggy shoreline less than twenty meters away. He walked the rest of the way before finding a spot well beyond the approaching tide and began digging. Once he scooped out a hole deep enough to hide his gear, he headed toward the prison where the asset was located.

According to Black's briefing, Capt. Trevor Watkins went missing when his F-22 malfunctioned and crashed just off the coast of Russia. However, he was rescued by a Russian destroyer, which detained him for further questioning. Six months had elapsed and the Russian military had yet to acknowledge that they had Watkins. But Black didn't always trust his briefings. The only thing he believed for certain was that an American pilot was being held captive. And Black was tasked with breaking out the captain from a Russian military detention center and taking him home.

J.D. Blunt, who oversaw the Firestorm program, was somber when describing the mission. "It's damn near impossible," he had told Black. "You sure you still want to do this? I can always tell the Air Force to handle their own mess."

Black shook his head. "I can handle it." The fact that the Air Force Special Forces unit saw this as a suicide mission was all Black needed to know to sign up. His secret death wish wasn't so secret—and every superior who learned this about Black took advantage of that information. Black liked it that way.

After transitioning into more appropriate attire for the mountainous terrain ahead of him, Black turned his coms back on.

"Made it off the beach," he announced.

"It's about time," Shields said. "I was starting to wonder if you'd stopped to build a sandcastle."

"That's a sore subject," Black said. "Can we not mention that again?"

"Aww," Shields said softly. "Did a big wave sweep away your creation?"

"No," Black said tersely. "My stepdad stomped on it when part of my wall started to crumble."

She was silent for a few seconds before responding. "Sorry about that. I didn't know I was inviting a therapy session with my comment."

"You're not inviting anything, because I don't ever wanna talk about it."

Black had never spoken about it with anyone. And since it didn't even rank in the list of the top one thousand things his stepfather did to him, he figured there wouldn't be much point in it. But Black didn't talk about any of the thousand things in the list either. It was easier to deal with it that way.

Picking his way up the sloping mountain, he went over how he might handle the volatile and fluid situation he was about to encounter. He'd look for opportunities to eliminate guards and sneak onto the compound without attracting any attention. That was the key to success. If they didn't see him until he'd already freed Capt. Watkins, they would have the advantage necessary to survive the ensuing onslaught.

The prison was part of a larger military installation and positioned on a clearing near the top of one of Kamchatka's soaring peaks. According to intel reports, the Russians used the location as a staging area for intelligence ops as well as detaining political prisoners. Devoid of any guard towers, the base relied on its well-trained personnel to handle any potential issues.

With the facility surrounded by boulders and a barbed-wire perimeter fence, Black needed to get over it without touching it. But the degree of difficulty was increased due to the dusting of snow that had fallen in the upper elevations earlier that evening. Black slipped as he tested his footing on one of the rocks, but he didn't see any other viable options.

Placing his feet on the rock again, he squatted before pushing upward with a powerful leap. He nearly cleared the barbed wire at the top, but the edge of his pants snagged, which jerked him back into the fence. Black's face slapped hard against the cold metal links before he tumbled to the ground. The noise set off an alarm and sent guards scurrying in his direction.

So much for the element of surprise.

Black scrambled to his feet and raced toward a nearby shed for cover. He peeked around the corner and listened in on the conversation between the three soldiers who had arrived there. One of them shined his flashlight on the fence and noticed a torn piece of fabric, resulting in the trio spreading out and scanning the area.

Black cursed under his breath, but it was loud enough for Shields to hear it.

"You in some trouble?" she asked.

"It wouldn't be any fun if I wasn't," Black whispered.

"I'm watching this on satellite right now, and I think you might be able to cause a diversion with that tanker sitting just beyond the building opposite of your location."

"Roger that."

Black first needed to handle the nearby soldier. As he crept closer, Black affixed a silencer to the nozzle of his gun before firing a headshot. The man crumpled to the ground, and then Black dragged the body behind the shed before anyone could see him.

According to the schematics and intel the military had gathered, the building serving as a prison was right in front of him and Watkins was most likely in the far back, which was closest to Black. But first he had to create a diversion in the front.

When the two guards were out of sight, Black raced toward the building. He leaped up and then latched on to a drainage pipe running down the side of the wall. After shimmying his way to the top, Black wormed across the roof. He identified the tanker and proceeded to hurl two timed explosives underneath the vehicle. Without waiting for them to blow, he returned to the back of the building and waited.

Three . . . two . . . one . . .

The first explosion rocked the compound, sending soldiers scurrying outside toward the truck now engulfed in flames.

He jumped to the ground and placed another device on the back wall, synching it up with the second device by the tanker on the other side. Once that was finished, he raced to the shed to take cover.

And now . . .

The simultaneous explosions turned the Russian military installation into ground zero for chaos. Dressed in his Russian guard attire, he tugged his hat down low and raced back toward the smoldering building. Picking his way through the rubble, he entered the back of the holding cell, which was full of shell-shocked prisoners. One of the men was running toward the freshly opened hole before he came to an immediate stop when his gaze met Black's. Black nodded toward the hole, a gesture that the man took as permission to escape. He resumed his attempt at freedom and jumped through the opening.

Black scanned the room for Watkins and found him crouched against a sidewall, wide-eyed, as he watched the unfolding scene. The three-inch scar on the right side of his face made him easy to identify.

"Captain Watkins, come with me," Black said as he strode over to the American.

"What's happening?" Watkins asked.

"Just come with me, and keep your mouth shut," Black said before slapping a pair of handcuffs on Watkins.

Black guided Watkins out through the back, and they walked around the side of the building. Soldiers scurried in and out as they tried to put out the fire. More prisoners followed the first fearless man's attempt and started pouring out of the back and scaling the fence. Black and Watkins were nearly invisible as they meandered calmly through the frenetic activity.

After a brief search, Black located a Jeep with the keys in the ignition. He ordered Watkins inside, keeping up the charade that he was a Russian soldier. The ruse was working so well that Watkins still didn't seem to know who Black was.

"Where are you taking me?" Watkins asked.

Black flashed a wry smile. "I'm getting you out of here."

Watkins grabbed Black's arm. "Who said I want to leave?"

"We don't really have time for this," Black said as he turned the key, igniting the engine.

"Sorry you went through all this trouble, but I'd rather stay."

"You'd rather stay in a remote Russian prison?" Black asked with a furrowed brow. "I believe this might be the worst case of Stockholm syndrome I've ever come across."

"It's not Stockholm syndrome. I just know who

you're taking me back to—and those people are going to kill me."

"Not as long as you're with me."

Watkins tightened his grip on Black's arm. "You can't protect me forever."

He glanced down at Watkins's hand. "I suggest you let go of me so we can get out of here."

Black eased onto the gas and made his way toward the gate.

"I'll tell the guard who you are," Watkins said. "I'm not going back."

Black stopped the vehicle and glared at Watkins. "You're going to keep your mouth shut or else I'll shut it for you."

"*Pomogite!*" Watkins shouted as he leaned out of the Jeep and tried to get the attention of a nearby soldier.

Black snatched a fistful of Watkins's collar and yanked him back inside before head butting him. Watkins squawked in pain before Black slammed his asset's head into the dashboard, knocking him out.

The guard cocked his head to one side as he stared at them.

Black sneered as he looked at the soldier. "Americans!" With a shrug, Black threw the Jeep into gear and motored toward the exit. When he arrived at the gate, an armed guard asked to see Black's papers.

Black acted as if he was going to hand the man something but instead produced a gun. "*Otkryt' vorota!*"

The soldier didn't need to be told twice as he followed Black's command and activated the gate. Black hit the man with two shots in the chest before speeding out of the base.

The Jeep bounced along the rugged road, racing toward the base of the mountain.

"I've got the asset," Black said into his coms.

"Nice work," Shields said. "You only had to set fire to the mountain to do it."

"Let's focus on the results here. I have Watkins in my possession."

"And is he excited to be going home?"

Black huffed a laugh through his nose. "No, this flyboy is messed up. He begged me to stay."

"Are you kidding me?"

"I wish I was. I had to knock him out to keep him from ruining my escape plan. He was going on and on about how someone was going to kill him and how I couldn't protect him."

"Well, you're going to need to hurry because you've got company."

Black cursed again as he downshifted and swung around a tight corner. He saw the first glint of a headlight in his rearview mirror, confirming what Shields said.

"I'll take care of him," Black said. "You just make sure everything is ready to go at the extraction point."

"Roger that."

Black accelerated out of the curve and skidded around the next one. Then he put the Jeep in park and jumped out. He ran around to the passenger side to drag Watkins onto the ground and hide him behind a boulder. Next, Black found a large rock and ran back to the Jeep. He climbed inside and shifted into gear before placing the rock on top of the accelerator. Black hustled over to Watkins and waited for the pursuing vehicle to appear. A few seconds later, the Russians came around the corner in time to see the Jeep plummet off the side.

The soldiers got out to inspect the damage. When they did, Black opened fire, taking out both men. He hurled their bodies over the cliff as they landed on top of the burning Jeep. Easing behind their vehicle's steering wheel, he headed back up the hill to get Watkins.

A Range Rover. This is quite the upgrade.

Watkins staggered to his feet and started to run once he made eye contact with Black. However, the asset didn't get more than a few steps before Black tackled him.

"I told you I'm getting you out of here," Black said as he subdued Watkins with a bear hug. "And I always keep my promises."

Black spun Watkins around and punched him again, rendering him unconscious.

"I think we're all clear here," Black said over his coms. "Any sign of more bogeys?"

"You're good," Shields said.

"And the extraction team?"

"Ready and waiting. But I suggest you hurry before the Russians figure out what you just did."

Black chuckled. "They'll be scratching their heads about this one for days."

"Let's hope so. In the meantime, I'm gonna do a little digging on Watkins and see what I can find out. I've never heard of any of our soldiers wanting to stay in a Russian prison."

"It does seem odd, doesn't it?"

"Odd doesn't begin to describe that response to a rescue. But good work, Black."

"Just another day at the beach."

CHAPTER 2

Two years earlier
Benoa Bay, Bali
Indonesia

TATIANA'S EYES WIDENED, and her mouth fell agape as she dug her toes into the sand. She spun around and threw her hands up. After running toward the ocean for a few meters, she stopped and closed her eyes. With a deep breath, she inhaled the saltwater air and smiled.

"Mama, this is amazing," she said, using her native Russian tongue.

Her mother nodded knowingly, her expression stoic. "It sure is, isn't it?"

"I thought Papa said he'd never be able to take off enough time to make a holiday trip like this."

"That's what he said, but your Papa is full of surprises."

Tatiana absorbed the afternoon sunshine, pausing for a moment to bask in her good fortune. In a week, she'd turn thirteen and begin studying at a special sports academy for gifted athletes in Moscow. Despite applying without either of her parents' knowledge, she was pleased when they both agreed to let her attend the school and pursue her dream of representing Russia in the Olympics. Losing a few privileges for a month as a punishment for forging her parents' signature was well worth it.

"Is Papa going to join us?" she asked.

"He promised that he'd be along soon," her mother said. "He had a few phone calls to make for business."

Tatiana shrugged. She was accustomed to her father's absence after years of him working as a traveling salesman for a natural gas company. He was dedicated to his job, so much so that it was common for him to field a business-related request during dinner. And while her mother complained about it incessantly, Tatiana never did. She appreciated the fact that he provided for them, even if it meant never taking trips as a family.

Until now.

Tatiana waded into the ocean, bobbing up and down with the waves. She slapped at the water and giggled. After a minute, she leaned into a wave and floated on her back, wishing her brother Peter could've been with her. He always talked about going to the seaside, though she doubted he would've ever imagined Bali being the destination. Yalta or Sochi, maybe. But Bali would've been out of the question since it required a plane trip to get there. And while her father made a better living than most, he still would've been apprehensive based on the cost. His penny-pinching ways often resulted in shouting matches between her parents. However, when he announced this trip, he said it was a special one, made possible because he had an assignment in Bali.

Tatiana retreated to the beach and spread out her blanket before deciding what book to read. When she looked around and didn't see her father, she pulled out her copy of The Hunger Games. He vocalized his displeasure whenever he saw her reading English books, and he would be especially upset with her selection due to the violent nature of the story.

But if he isn't here . . .

Tatiana read for an hour straight without a word to her mother.

"Is Papa ever going to join us?" Tatiana asked. His absence is what emboldened her to quit ballet a year ago and take up playing soccer. He stormed around the house when her mother told him about it, but she told him she'd only continue dancing if he took her to practice. That ended the discussion.

"I told you that he said he'd be along soon, but I

also told you he's full of surprises."

Her lips eased into a smile. "You think he has something special planned for us?"

"That'll be the day," her mother said sarcastically as she stroked Tatiana's straight blonde locks.

Tatiana rolled her eyes and scanned the beach. While she had been engrossed in her novel, she noticed a handful of kids around her age were in the water and playing games. She slammed the book shut and leaped to her feet. Tossing her phone to her mother, Tatiana ran toward the ocean.

"I'm going to go play with those kids," she shouted back over her shoulder.

Tatiana's boldness meant she never lacked for friends, something she trained herself to do after Peter vanished.

"Tatiana, you come back here right now," her mother called.

Tatiana spun around to face her mother but continued moving backward. "I'll be fine. I'm right here, so you'll be able to see me the whole time."

She leaped over a little boy's sandcastle and sprinted into the water. There were three boys and two girls tossing a ball around in what appeared to be a game of keep away. One of the girls, Allison, introduced Tatiana to everyone before immediately placing her in the middle. Their thick English accents and pale skin easily gave away their nationality. The other kids could only get the ball over her head once before she soared out of the water and snatched it.

"Wow," one of the boys said. "Are you some sort of superhero?"

Tatiana chuckled. "I play keeper—and one day you'll cheer for me."

"For England?" he asked, his eyes still wide in disbelief.

"Do I look English?" she asked, eyeing him closely.

"Well, you don't sound it, but you could've fooled me if I hadn't heard you talk."

She shrugged. "Does it matter who I play for?"

The boy shook his head. "You're bloody amazing."

Tatiana smiled, soaking in the complement. In less than half an hour, she became instant friends with the kids, who were part of three families traveling together from London. Once they stopped playing, they bounced in the water and started talking.

"Do you come here often?" Tatiana asked Allison.

"Every year," she said. "It's a tradition. Our fathers all work together."

"What do they do?"

Allison sighed. "I don't know. Some boring

business stuff, I think."

One of the boys, Michael, interrupted their conversation. "Who wants to get some ice cream? My treat."

The kids shouted with delight.

"What about you, Tatiana?" Michael asked. "Would you like to join us?"

She hesitated, weighing what she wanted to do with what she knew her mother would say. "I—I don't think so."

"Oh, come on. Don't be a spoil sport. We're just going to walk about a half a mile over there and get a little snack before supper."

She looked across the water and saw the sun starting to slip below the horizon. But she didn't say a word.

"Well," Michael said, "what's it gonna be?"

"I promised my mother that I'd watch the sunset with her," she said glancing toward her mother, whose head was tilted back and mouth open while apparently asleep.

"Is that her there?" he asked, pointing at her mother.

Tatiana nodded.

"I think she forgot," Michael said. "Come on. It won't hurt if you come with us."

She sighed. "Okay."

"Yes," Allison said, hugging Tatiana from behind. "You won't regret it. This place has the most amazing ice cream outside of the British Empire."

"Well, that makes sense since this was part of our Empire at one time," Michael said.

Allison slapped him on the arm as they trudged ashore. "Didn't you ever pay attention in geography during primary school? The Dutch colonized this part of Indonesia."

Michael shrugged. "It's still delicious no matter who once ruled here."

Tatiana tagged along with the group until they reached the ice cream parlor. She struggled to understand half of what they were talking about. The way they talked, she wondered if London was on another planet.

"So, you're a keeper?" Michael asked.

Tatiana nodded.

"Who's your favorite player in the Premier League?"

"In the what?" she asked.

"Leave her alone, Michael," Allison said, punching him in the arm. "Not everyone is so obsessed with football like you are."

The lights over the shop flickered on as the sun dipped below the horizon. They all discussed what they were going to order and waited patiently. When they all had a cone in hand, Allison proposed a toast.

"Here's to new friends," Allison said, throwing her arm around Tatiana's shoulder.

"To new friends," they all said in unison, hoisting their desserts in the air.

A boy walked by, half-heartedly dribbling a soccer ball. Michael raced over to him and stole it away with some fancy footwork without any protests. The younger boy tried to take it back but couldn't hold his own against the English teen.

"Just a moment," Michael said to the boy. "I want to see if this girl is as good as she says she is. I'll give your ball right back."

The boy shrugged and nodded permissively.

"Give your cone to Allison, and line up between those two tables," Michael said, directing Tatiana where to go. "Those look about the right distance for a goal, don't you agree?"

"Sure," Tatiana said as she took her place and crouched into her stance.

"Ready?" Michael asked.

She flashed him a thumbs up sign and prepared for his shot. He backed up a few feet and raced toward the ball. Striking low and leaning back, Michael lifted the ball well over what would've been the crossbar and flying toward the street.

"Show off," Allison said. "Go get the ball."

"I'll get it," Tatiana said.

"No, make Michael do it. That was an atrocious penalty shot."

"I don't mind, really," Tatiana said before turning to fetch the ball.

She saw the ball bouncing across the street and waited for a few cars to stop and allow her to pass through the crosswalk. When she reached the other side, she looked up and saw a man in a suit with his foot on the ball next to a dark SUV.

"May I have that ball, sir?" Tatiana asked.

The man eyed her cautiously before offering the ball just in front of him with his foot. When she went to pick it up, two men jumped out of the vehicle and shoved her into the backseat. She was so caught off guard by their actions that she didn't scream until she was almost all the way inside. The doors slammed shut as Tatiana continued to scream.

One of the men in the back pulled out a gun. "You'll shut up if you know what's good for you," he said in Russian.

She narrowed her eyes, glaring at him.

The man outside picked the ball up and booted it back toward the kids and waved. He got inside and drove off.

Tatiana looked over her shoulder, trying to see if her new friends comprehended what was happening.

They didn't appear alarmed, just somewhat confused by her disappearance as they stood there apparently awaiting her return.

"Why are you doing this to me?" she demanded, reverting to her native tongue.

None of the men said a word as they sped along alleyways and darted through intersections. She was making copious notes in her head, trying to see if she could remember where she was going. Then she felt a sudden prick in the side of her neck. She glanced at the guard sitting to her right, and he smiled and snickered. A few seconds later, Tatiana lost consciousness.

* * *

TATIANA AWOKE some time later on a cot in a cell in the middle of a warehouse. She wasn't sure how long she'd been out, but she had a searing headache. After rubbing her eyes, she scanned the room and tried to gather her wits. There was another girl about her age huddled in the corner.

"Hey," Tatiana shouted. "I demand to know what's going on!"

The other girl looked up. "Don't say another word. It's not worth it."

Tatiana glanced at her new roommate, who sported a large shiner around her right eye.

"Did they do this to you?" Tatiana asked.

The girl nodded slowly. "And they'll do it to you too if you continue shouting."

Tatiana ignored the girl. "Hello? Anyone? I demand to know why you've brought me here right now."

A guard stormed toward her cell and unlocked it. He strode up to Tatiana before shoving her against the wall.

"One more outburst like that and you'll regret it," he said as he sneered at her.

"Oh, really?" Tatiana said. She took a deep breath and shouted again. "Tell me why I'm here."

The guard pinned her against the wall, pressing his nightstick against her throat. "This is your last chance. Understand?"

She gasped for breath, grabbing for her throat as she tried to breathe.

"Understand?" the guard asked again.

Tatiana strained to nod before the guard released her. She crumpled to the ground, coughing and heaving as she tried to regain her breath. Her cellmate waited until the man left before rushing over.

"Are you okay?" the girl asked.

Tatiana glanced up to make sure they were alone before nodding. Then she dug a cell phone out of her pocket.

"He did exactly what I wanted him to," she said.

Once she sat up, she dialed her mother's cell phone number. The call went straight to voicemail. She hung up and entered her father's number before pressing the "send" button.

"Allo," he said after answering.

"Papa," Tatiana said, "some men took me while I was at the beach. Please, I need your help."

He didn't say a word.

"Papa!" she cried. "Say something."

Still nothing.

"Papa, it's me. Tatiana."

The line went dead.

CHAPTER 3

Tangier, Morocco

J.D. BLUNT STOOD TO GREET Capt. Watkins
with a handshake as Black ushered the former Russian
captive into the cozy living room. After the trio
exchanged pleasantries, they all sat down, taking in the
surroundings of the Firestorm safe house. The
windows were open, allowing the breeze from the
Mediterranean to cool the place.

"Sorry about the delay in getting you home,"
Blunt said as he swirled his glass of bourbon. "I
wanted to hear the truth straight from your mouth."

"I don't know whether to punch you or thank
you for rescuing me," Watkins said.

"Well, I'm not responsible for saving you," Blunt
said as he pointed at Black. "That guy right there is
the one who did all the hard work."

"Yeah, and I still have a massive headache
because of him."

"But at least your life is not subject to the whims of a Russian general."

"Russian general, American base commander—what's the difference?"

Blunt took a long pull on his drink. "I hope they're not one in the same, but let's hear it."

Watkins scanned the room. "Can I have a drink first?"

"Of course," Blunt said. "Where are my manners?"

He eased out of his chair and shuffled across the room to the wet bar on the far wall. "I have bourbon and scotch. Which do you prefer?"

"Bourbon, neat."

"I knew I liked you," Blunt said.

Watkins drummed his fingers on the arm of the chair while he waited for his drink. "Is this how you debrief all the people you rescue?"

Blunt chuckled. "Hardly. Your case is a rare one, though not completely unprecedented. However, I know the feeling. My own government has tried to kill me too."

"What'd you do about it?"

"I faked my death."

"That's what I wished you would've let me do," Watkins said before taking a swig of his bourbon.

"Well, tell me your story, and Agent Black and I will see what we can do to keep you safe."

Watkins took a deep breath. "Where to begin? Let's see."

"It's your story," Blunt said. "Tell it however you like."

Watkins drained the rest of his glass before continuing. "I'm not sure how comfortable I am divulging all the details."

"Just tell us what you know," Blunt said.

"Well, my suspicion is based on the fact that my base commander—"

"Isn't that Gil Roman?" Blunt asked.

Watkins nodded and continued. "Colonel Roman asked me to fly a reconnaissance mission over the Stanovoy Mountains near a suspected missile launch site the Russian military was constructing."

Black furrowed his brow. "Air recon in Russia?"

"We don't need to do it very often anymore," Watkins said. "But it's not so rare that I would question it right off the bat. And the assignment was simple. I was supposed to fly over this location and gather intel—pictures, radio activity, radiation levels— standard fare for that type of operation. According to Roman, the facility was carved out of rock and we needed better imagery than what we were getting with our satellites."

"Sounds like a straightforward recon mission," Blunt said.

"That's what I thought—until I reached the site," Watkins said. "I should've been able to zip in and out before they knew I was there. But it's like they were waiting on me. One of their surface-to-air missiles locked in on my position, but I was able to roll away at the last second to avoid getting blown out of the sky. However, my fuselage got hit by some artillery fire from the ground, and I had to bail out."

"How long did it take them to find you?" Black asked.

"They were waiting for me before my feet touched the dirt. I was surrounded and just threw my hands in the air, praying they didn't shoot me. There were two high-ranking commanders on site. One of them was arguing to kill me, while the other one insisted that I needed to be interrogated. After a few minutes of deliberation, they forced me into the back of one of their transport units with three soldiers. A couple days later, they transferred me to their installation on the Kamchatka Peninsula, and I stayed there until you extracted me."

"Extracted against your will, I might add," Black said.

Watkins narrowed his eyes, ignoring Black's comment. "There's no way that missile site could've foreseen an aerial reconnaissance mission, much less armed for it unless they knew I was coming. Someone had to have tipped them off. And I think it was Roman."

"Do you have any other reason to think he was the one who did this to you?" Blunt asked.

Watkins looked down and sighed, pausing before answering. "Not really. It's just a general feeling I get about him that he doesn't like me. I don't think he appreciates how much of a stickler I am for making sure everything is done with precision."

"That doesn't sound like him," Blunt said. "From what I remember of Roman, he's a standup guy who'll do anything for his men—and he runs a tight ship."

"Maybe that's how he was back in the day, but now he's just another career military man trying to climb the ranks to the Pentagon so he can retire with a fat pension and get a cushy consulting gig."

Blunt chuckled. "Washington's crawling with those vermin. You don't wanna get me started."

"So you get what I'm talking about, don't you?"

Blunt nodded. "Unfortunately, all too well."

"Roman had to be the one to do it since he said the mission was top secret. He even told me not to fill out a flight plan. Everything was set up for me to disappear."

"Perhaps you're right."

Watkins's jaw fell agape. "Perhaps? If this isn't solid proof that he tried to get me killed, I don't know what is. Now, let me ask you a question: Are you a religious man?"

"I grew up Baptist, if that means anything to you," Blunt said.

"Good," Watkins said. "I know you'll understand this analogy then. Do you remember the story in the Bible about King David and Bathsheba?"

"How can I forget? Who doesn't enjoy a good unrequited love story?"

Watkins wagged his finger. "Only it wasn't unrequited. David sent Bathsheba's husband Uriah to the front lines of battle, knowing he would die and then Bathsheba could be added to David's growing list of wives."

"That's why you never bathe naked on the rooftop," Black added.

"There are plenty of good nuggets of wisdom nestled in that story, but the point I'm trying to make is that there are ways to get rid of people you don't like without making it look like you're doing it. I will guarantee you that Roman never thought I'd return."

Blunt clipped off the end of one of his cigars and stuffed the stogie into his mouth. He chewed on the tobacco while he considered the story.

"Well, what do you think?" Watkins asked, breaking the silence.

"It's conceivable that you're reading too much into this," Blunt said.

Watkins shook his head. "But not likely. What are

the odds that I would return considering how he stacked the deck against me?"

Blunt leaned forward, scooting to the edge of his chair. "Look, I'm not trying to dismiss what you're saying, but I do know that sometimes when we think something is there, we look hard for it. And to be frank with you, I'm an evidence guy. And if I'm going to take some kind of action against Col. Roman or others on the leadership of your base, I better have proof in hand of what's going on and their efforts to silence you. Conjecture and circumstantial evidence aren't enough for me to levy this kind of charge."

"I understand your point," Watkins said, "but why was I left at that base for so long? I think the only reason anyone knew I was missing was because some relentless reporter wrote an article about me. Then they couldn't just ignore it."

"They could if they really wanted to," Blunt said. "They could've concocted some cover story that would've explained everything, and it would've all gone away. But the military needed a big win after a spell of bad PR. This was an easy victory they can now claim."

"Why did they call you instead of sending in a SEAL team or Air Force Special Ops?" Watkins asked. "We have guys who train their whole lives for these missions and never get tasked with extracting a pilot behind enemy lines. Yet someone at the Pentagon called you, the leader of some black ops program I've never heard of, to handle it. This doesn't add up, and I'm hoping you look through all the fog and see what I'm talking about."

Blunt stood. "I want to help you Capt. Watkins, but I have the feeling you're either conspiratorial in nature or you're not telling me everything. Now, which is it?"

"When I'm dead, you'll know I was right—but it'll be too late by then," Watkins said, pointing at Blunt. "My blood will be on your hands too. I hope you can live with that."

Blunt offered his hand. "We're going to do everything in our power to make sure that doesn't happen."

Watkins ignored Blunt's gesture. "And how are you going to do that?"

"I'll have some of my people look into it."

"If you don't take action now, it's not going to do me any good."

"Unfortunately, I'm not the president, so I can't make unilateral decisions and get to the bottom of everything. But I promise you that I will try and do so posthaste."

Watkins huffed. "I guess I'll take what I can get."

Black escorted Watkins out of the safe house, leaving Blunt alone to his thoughts. He wanted to believe Watkins, but the story seemed entirely circumstantial. After ruminating for a few minutes, he picked up his phone and dialed Shields's number.

"I need you to do me a favor," he said.

"What do you need?" she asked.

"Get me a full work up on Captain Trevor Watkins. I want to know everything about this guy we just rescued."

CHAPTER 4

Two years earlier

TATIANA AWOKE WITH a gasp followed by a harsh bump to her forehead. Her attempt to sit up in the dark was foiled—and she wasn't sure by what. She tried to move her arms, but couldn't more than a few inches due to the hard walls on both sides of her. Realizing she was confined to a tight space, she screamed and kicked, anything to get help. After a few seconds, she hyperventilated. She wasn't sure what she was in, but she couldn't figure any way out

After a half-minute, she steadied her breathing and tried to regain her composure.

It's going to be all right. It's going to be all right.

The space beneath her vibrated, and a constant dull hum emanated from somewhere outside. Still trying to figure out where she was, she banged her head on the space just above her.

I'm in a box on an airplane? At least I'm not dead.

The last thing she remembered was eating breakfast at the prison with her cellmate. Everything was fuzzy after that. Her head ached, and her muscles were cramping.

They drugged me.

That was the only logical explanation since she couldn't recall ever walking onto a jet voluntarily. But how big was it? Were all the other young teens she'd seen in the warehouse here too? Was her cellmate here? A thousand more questions flooded Tatiana's mind, and she gladly entertained them. Anything to forget about the betrayal from her father. But that wasn't easy to do.

Why didn't he say anything when he answered the phone? Did he have something to do with this?

Her mind raced as she tried to come up with a rational reason for why her father didn't respond.

Maybe the connection was bad. That had to be it. He probably didn't even hear me.

That's what she wanted to believe. She adored her father, even though he wasn't around much. Her mother made snide comments about him all the time, about his travel schedule and his general absence at important family functions. He even missed his own mother's birthday party for three years running, forcing Tatiana's mother to go alone. And she despised her mother in law.

But deep down, Tatiana knew something wasn't right. Her father was supposed to come down to the beach after he'd finished work. And he never showed up. At the very least, he would text or call. She considered the possibility that he had while she was in the water or off getting ice cream with her friends, yet she couldn't shake the eerie sense that he was involved in this, whatever this was.

About an hour later, the plane bounced and the tires barked as it landed. She guessed about half an hour had elapsed since coming to a full stop before she heard voices. Then, seconds later, a whooshing noise along with mist began to fill her box.

* * *

TATIANA DIDN'T KNOW how long she was knocked out, but when she regained consciousness, she was lying on a concrete floor in a well-lit warehouse. The muggy air hung thick around her. A pair of soldiers armed with machine guns stood guarding the exit along the far wall. As she continued to survey her surroundings, she whipped around to look at the opposite wall and saw two more men toting weapons.

A cool breeze wafted through the building, bringing temporary respite from the humid conditions. But once the wind dissipated, sweat beaded on her forehead.

One of the guards noticed that she was awake and shouted at another man before pointing at her. He acknowledged the report with a head nod and strode over to Tatiana.

"Welcome back, Tatiana," the man said in Russian. "You were out for quite a while."

"Where am I? What is this place?" she demanded.

"You're safe now," he said, placing his hand on the small of her back. "And I'm going to make sure you never get in a situation like that again."

"What kind of situation was I in?"

The man patted her on the head in a patronizing fashion. "Oh, Tatiana, you have so much to learn about the world."

"Why don't you start the first lesson by telling me who you are and what I'm doing here."

"Just relax, Tatiana," he said as he stood. "You're going to enjoy yourself here as long as you do as you're told."

CHAPTER 5

TITUS BLACK LIFTED the coffee lid and tossed it into the trash. He eased his face over the steam and inhaled. Given the long day of travel he'd endured after meeting with Capt. Watkins, Black needed something to rouse him from his drowsy state. He lumbered to the back of the coffee shop and then settled into a booth, the perfect position to watch both the front door and the news anchor introducing a piece about the Ukrainian government.

Black shifted in his seat and listened intently to the story. The reporter on location gave a brief primer on the tense relations between Russia and the Ukraine before switching to a clip of Ukrainian President Vasyl Petrenko in front of a podium at a press conference. With an easel to his left, he pointed to a simplified diagram explaining how the new Ukrainian missile defense system would halt any future attacks from

Russia. According to Petrenko, no longer would the Russian military be able to target the Ukrainian people at will. The new technology was designed to neutralize such threats before they had an opportunity to inflict any damage.

The translator for the report reworded Petrenko's speech: "No longer will we cower in fear at the Russian bullies on our doorstep. They will need to focus their efforts elsewhere as we have the ability to thwart anything our neighbors try to assault us with. The Ukraine will survive as a democratic state determined to play a significant role in world politics."

Black chuckled at Petrenko's bluster. If the Ukrainian president could get away with annihilating Russia, he would. And he wouldn't think twice about it.

Moments later, Nate Miller, *The Washington Post* reporter responsible for breaking the story that initiated the extraction request for Capt. Watkins, strode through the door.

"Mr. Miller," Black said as he stood and gave a polite wave to the newsman.

Miller turned and walked over to Black's table. "Thank you for meeting me, sir. Senator Blunt spoke very highly of you, though he didn't tell me your name. He just said I should meet with one of his team members about that article and see if there's more to it."

"It's best that you don't know my name, for your sake and for mine."

"Okay. You value your privacy. I can appreciate that."

Black nodded. "Can I buy you something to drink? Coffee?"

"Coffee, and I'll take it black," Miller said.

"The reporter's special," Black said with a wink. He walked to the counter and placed an order for Miller.

Once the two men settled into their chairs, Black opened the meeting.

"I appreciate your willingness to share your experience with me," Black said. "I'm always intrigued by the people who break big stories."

"Well, I don't wear a cape or anything like that. If you're looking for some kind of superhero, you need to keep looking."

"No, no, no," Black said with a wave of his hand. "I'm just interested in learning more about what inspired you to start digging into this story."

Miller sighed before taking a long sip of his drink. "To be honest with you, I'm beginning to wonder if that was the right thing to do."

"What do you mean?"

"For starters, I was nearly killed last week when some maniac ran me off the road."

Black forced a smile. "Welcome to Washington."

"No, I've lived here for a while. I know what it's like to drive on the beltway every day. This wasn't some random incident where I cut some guy off and he was ticked at me. No, this was very deliberate."

"Are you sure? People in Washington can be temperamental."

"Positive," Miller said. "The guy nudged me off the road, and I spun out. My car hit a tree near a park, but I fortunately didn't hit my head and maintained consciousness. My door was jammed, so I crawled out the passenger side before the vehicle burst into flames."

"Burst into flames after hitting a tree?"

"I heard some sort of sound like a rocket maybe right after I got out. The next thing I know, my car was obliterated."

"By an RPG?"

"I don't know about all your military acronyms. I just know I wasn't supposed to survive."

"What'd you tell the cops?"

"Nothing," Miller said. "I kept my mouth shut and returned to my normal job. To be honest, I love breaking stories, but not at the expense of my life. Of all the accolades I could win from my friends, I'd hate to not be there to receive it. Posthumous awards aren't exactly what I'm striving for."

Black nodded. "That's understandable. But to get a response like that, you had to ruffle a few feathers. What else do you know that you're not telling me?"

Miller shook his head. "I have no idea. Everything I learned that I could verify was in the initial story. From what I could tell, the military was ignoring Capt. Watkins and planned on leaving him to rot in a Russian prison."

"Do you think the Air Force didn't consider Watkins someone worth rescuing?"

"I don't know. That's not my call. I just report facts—and the facts were that Watkins was shot down behind enemy lines and needed to be rescued in some form or fashion. I didn't care if it was through a Navy SEAL extraction team or some black ops agent. I just know he should've at least been regarded enough as a high value member of our military to go retrieve. These days it seems like we're so focused on the overall geopolitical landscape that we forget what we're really about."

"And what are we really about, Mr. Miller?"

"Should we be about caring for each person, no matter what flag they're draped in? Isn't that what our military does through its humanitarian missions and other global operations?"

Black chuckled and shook his head. "I honestly wish that were the case, but that's not the world we live in. Our soldiers know the risk they face every time they suit up for a mission. And sometimes the fallout isn't pretty."

"I understand that, but there's always more to the story," Miller said, tapping his pen on the table.

"Is that what you were hoping for today? That I would tell you the rest of the story?"

Miller shrugged. "Maybe not for print."

"You want me to give you a peek behind the curtains and think that you're not going to broadcast it to the world?"

"Do you trust me?"

Black eyed him closely. "I haven't decided yet. But I'm starting to get the idea that there's more to your story that you're not telling me. Perhaps the real question is do you trust me?"

"I'm not sure I can trust anyone because there are a lot of things in my world right now that aren't making much sense after I published that article."

"What did you expect when you started this? That you would just smack the hornet's nest and escape without getting swarmed? You're dealing with some powerful people, the kind who don't appreciate you shedding light on all their dealings in the dark."

Miller sighed. "So what are you going to do about it? Isn't that what you do?"

"I'm not a superhero either. I have to operate

within the confines of the law just like everyone else."

"Except when you don't."

Black smiled wryly. "There are times when the situation calls for a little more heavy-handed use of force. Perhaps some people would say that what I do might push the boundaries of legality. But ultimately, it's not up to me to judge. I just do my best to follow orders."

"From where I'm sitting, you don't look like a robot," Miller quipped. "You should still be able to use some amount of discretion."

"And I do. But I can assure you there's nobody operating on the up-and-up that's firing RPGs at reporters."

"Exactly. And that's why I want you to find out who it is and stop them."

"So I can stop them? Or so you can write about them?"

Miller shrugged. "What difference does it make? These people need to be exposed. But for the record, I already told you I'm not looking for another story. I'm just trying to figure out who wants me dead."

"Well, if I could help you, I would. This is just as much of a mystery to us as it is to you. We're attempting to piece things together and figure out if there's more to tell."

"What do you mean? Like background information that I omitted?"

"Something like that."

Miller shook his head. "I told you it was all in that first story. Just a forgotten pilot who wasn't actually dead like the military initially told his family."

"And it's an intriguing article that I wished I'd read earlier."

"Why's that?"

"There was one detail that I found interesting and would've liked to have known before I debriefed the pilot. You said that he managed to sneak a letter out of prison to his parents. Did you see this letter?"

"Well, no, I didn't verify it, but they told me about it."

Black smiled. "I don't think he ever wrote a letter. I think that was a family suspicious about their son's death, and they got you to take the bait. Do you know how difficult it would be to get a stamp, write a letter, and mail it to the U.S. while in a Russian prison?"

Miller shook his head.

"Let's just put it this way," Black said. "It's easier to extract a hostage from there than it is to sneak out any type of correspondence."

"So you're saying the family fooled me?"

"Look, I know you might think that's some black mark against your journalistic integrity, but I'll never tell. And the end result is what you wanted, right? Bring a man back home? Can't argue with the results."

"Yeah, but now someone wants me dead. That's definitely not a result I intended."

"Hopefully you're safe now," Black said. "They might be counting on the fact that since you survived, you probably got the message."

"Are you sure about that?"

Black shook his head. "Not at all. I'd look into some self-defense classes and purchase a firearm for personal protection. If they send a professional after you, it may not matter, but at least you'll stand a fighting chance."

"So I'm screwed."

"If whoever is after you wants you dead, I'm not sure you can do much stop it. Just don't write a big exposé on military conspiracies, and keep your fingers crossed."

Miller sighed. "That's not real comforting."

"Would you rather me lie to you or shoot you straight?"

"There's no one else I can go to about this, is there?"

Black shook his head. "I'm afraid not. The police will think you're loony. And the military isn't exactly going to want to be your best friend after uncovering their lies. Besides, who knows how many organizations are connected to this attempted cover up of a missing pilot? It's best to let this sleeping dog lie."

Miller stood and offered his hand. "If you learn anything, please tell me. Blunt knows how to contact me."

"No promises, but if I learn who's behind it all, I'll tell you."

Black stepped outside and watched Miller walk away.

That's a dead man walking, and there's not a thing I can do about it.

CHAPTER 6

J.D. BLUNT GRIPPED the leather steering wheel of his BMW Series 8 coupe and headed north on I-95. He turned up the radio, blaring Rachmaninoff's Symphony No. 2 over the speakers. With all the turmoil he sifted through to make sense of his team's missions each day, the music soothed his mind, if only for a moment. He tried to relax but found it next to impossible as he pondered why the NSA director summoned him for an urgent meeting.

After flashing his credentials, the guard at the front of the facility waved Blunt through. Once inside the building, Blunt went through the standard security protocol before he found his way to the office of Sgt. Maj. Robert Besserman.

Besserman was relatively new to his appointment at the NSA and was one of the few people who knew about Firestorm, Blunt's secret black ops program. However, the agency's freshly minted director had an extensive background in intelligence while serving with the Army's Special Forces.

Blunt was ushered into the room by one of Besserman's assistants, who closed the door behind him after announcing Blunt's presence.

"J.D.," Besserman said with a wide grin as he strode across the room to greet Blunt. "It's so good to see you. I appreciate you coming down here on such short notice."

"Of course, anything for you, Bobby."

Besserman pointed to the chair across from his desk. "Please, have a seat."

Blunt sat down and glanced over at Besserman's wet bar in the corner of his office. "Still drinking scotch, I see."

"Of course. I'm just wondering when you're ever going to come around to drinking the good stuff."

"Kentucky makes the best liquor."

"My bottle of Macallan 1824 series begs to differ."

"This is why we can't ever decide on a good bar around here," Blunt said. "So, I know you didn't invite me out here to persuade me to drink scotch over bourbon. What's this visit all about?"

"Well, I've got a situation I wanted to read you in on and see if you might be able to help."

"I'll do my best."

Besserman opened up a folder on his desk and

glanced at it before looking up at Blunt. "Here's the deal. As you might know, Capt. Trevor Watkins is going to be speaking at a welcoming home ceremony tomorrow downtown. The president wanted to host it in the White House rose garden, but he's got some other business to attend to. So, he's asked Gaither to host the event."

"Senator Todd Gaither? That blowhard from Missouri?"

"That's the one. He's always causing trouble for somebody."

"So why did the president ask him?"

Besserman threw his hands in the air before leaning forward. "Don't ask me. I'm just the messenger here. Gaither certainly wouldn't have been my first choice. But maybe the president is attempting to show how he can bridge the partisan divide; I don't know."

"Meanwhile, Gaither is setting fire to every bridge he comes across."

"And that's sort of why you're here today."

"Gaither?"

"Well, I figured that you're still keeping an eye on Capt. Watkins since he returned from Russia, are you not?"

Blunt nodded. "He's staying in a secure location while he gets debriefed by every agency that wants a shot at learning something from his incarceration in a Russian military prison."

"From what I hear, nobody is getting much out of him."

"Yeah, he's a tight-lipped fellow. A little paranoid, if you ask me."

"So, Gaither has been getting a rash of death threats lately, a few that actually look somewhat credible. And I was hoping that you might have one of your agents scope out the location for the ceremony this afternoon to make sure there aren't any blindspots we're missing."

Blunt furrowed his brow. "There are other agencies who handle this sort of thing."

"I know. The FBI has several agents on the scene already, but your guys are the best. And since your agents might already be there . . ."

"Would it be so bad if Gaither got taken out?" Blunt asked with a wry smile. "Let's face it: the guy has made five times as many enemies as bills he's sponsored."

"Joking aside, our intelligence agencies don't need a black eye like this in what's already an embarrassing situation for the military. Besides, if Watkins is paranoid for good reason, it wouldn't be a bad idea to check it out so he has peace of mind as well."

Blunt stood and offered his hand. "If this request were coming from anyone else, I'd turn it down. But you know I'd do anything for you, Bobby."

"I appreciate it," Besserman said as he shook Blunt's hand. "I'll let the FBI know one of your agents will be putting another set of eyes on the site so they don't get jumpy."

"Excellent," Blunt said. "I'll keep you posted."

Blunt lumbered back to his car and wondered if Besserman was getting paranoid too. An on-site meeting at the NSA? Blunt could count on one hand the number of those he'd had.

Maybe there's more happening here than I know about.

CHAPTER 7

Two years earlier
Undisclosed location

TATIANA HAD NEVER been more self-conscious in her life than she was in the moment. Teens—both boys and girls—all about her age stood in single-file lines, exactly five feet apart from everyone to their left and right, front and back. She never considered herself good with estimating crowds but guessed that the group numbered somewhere around three hundred. Wearing just a white t-shirt and a white pair of shorts, she remained still, hands at her side, while the man in charge meandered his way through everyone, randomly looking each person up and down, sizing them up. Tatiana averted her eyes when he drew near to her.

"I like this one," he said in Russian, running his finger up Tatiana's neck and gently lifting her chin.

Seconds later, two men grabbed her by the arms and whisked her away. They stopped to speak with one of their superiors. Tatiana seized the opportunity to break away and make a run for it. She only got a few meters away before one of the guards recaptured her.

Crack!

The man belted her across the back with his cropping stick. "Demonstrate some respect," he said. "These men are here for your benefit. Don't treat them with contempt."

Tatiana grimaced and stood upright before continuing on, matching their pace. As they led her across the room, she heard the man everyone referred to as the "General" issue marching orders for several of the other teens.

After walking down a long corridor, she was escorted into a bunk room with two dozen beds. One of the men told her to find the bed with her name on it and to change into the clothes lying on the pillow.

Tatiana shuffled along and searched for her name. Apparently, she'd already been picked and the general was simply making a show of his selection process. She got dressed and was summarily joined by twenty-three other teenaged girls. Once everyone was situated, they lined up at the door in the order that they were chosen. Across the hall, there were two dozen boys following the same protocol.

One of the guards led them to a cafeteria and asked them to sit down and wait further instructions.

Tatiana hadn't had a warm meal in three days, and she could barely take her eyes off the scrumptious feast of fresh vegetables and meats piled high on each plate. A boy on the far end couldn't suppress his hunger any longer and picked up his eating utensils. He was about three bites into his meal before the general entered the room.

The only noise she could hear was the ominous clicking of the general's heels on the concrete floor and the scratching of silverware on the porcelain plate of the ravenous boy. He froze as the general strode right up to him.

"Is it good?" the man asked.

With bulging cheeks, the boy looked up and nodded.

"That makes me happy," the general said, pausing as the barrel-chested man with a neatly-cropped beard pulled out his gun from its holster. "At least you'll die having eaten one final good meal."

Without hesitating, he stuck the gun to the boy's head and pulled the trigger. He fell over backward and hit the ground with a sickening thud. As blood pooled around the kid, the general picked up a napkin and cleaned off his handgun before stepping nonchalantly over the body and pacing around the room.

"I saved that young man a lot of heartache," the general said. "However, I'm not a cruel person. The world is cruel—and it's my job to make sure you can handle all the evils you will encounter once you get out in it. Shooting poor Nicolai here also serves as a reminder that paying attention to your instructors' commands and obeying my direction is the only way you're going to survive, both in here and outside these walls."

One boy raised his hand, his lips quivering as he waited for permission to speak.

"Boris," the general said, pointing at the boy, "do you have a question?"

"Yes, sir."

"Proceed."

His voice quaked as he spoke. "Why exactly are we here? Are we being punished? Have we done something wrong?"

"Not at all. You're here because you're special, all of you. We've culled the best young people that our country has to offer and brought you together to make you better, to make you the best. You're going to make your country proud."

Boris raised his hand again.

"Did I not answer that sufficiently enough for you?" the general asked.

Boris swallowed hard. "Sir, I still don't know what you want us to do or our purpose for being here."

The general leaned down to get right up in the boy's face. "Did I stutter?"

He shook his head as he wrung his hands.

"Then what do you have a problem with?"

"I don't know, sir. I guess I'm wondering what you intend to do with us."

"Perhaps if you're not bright enough to figure that out from my previous reply, you're not as intelligent as we were led to believe," the general said before pulling out his gun again. He placed the nozzle against Boris's forehead and locked eyes with him.

"Would you like to ask me that question again, Boris?"

Boris took a deep breath, refusing to break eye contact with the man who could take his life. And instead of responding verbally, Boris leaned to his right while using both hands to swat at the weapon, pushing it away to the left. The sudden move caught the general off guard and knocked the gun free.

Not wanting to see any more blood shed, Tatiana dove for the gun, snatching it off the floor. She rolled over and popped up on her knees as the general pulled out a knife and put it to Boris's throat.

"That's enough," Tatiana said, training her gun on him.

The knife bounced when it hit the ground. It was a plastic prop.

The General smiled and offered his hand to Tatiana. She eyed him cautiously before taking it and rising to her feet.

"Mikhail," he said over his shoulder, "your role is complete. Please get up."

The boy who'd had his head shot stood and waved both his hands. "I'm fine."

"That'll be all," the general said, nodding toward the door.

Boris and Mikhail quickly exited the room while the lunatic leader paced around the tables. Tatiana sat down, her gaze fixed on the man now commanding the room's attention.

"Are you listening now?"

No one made a sound.

"The point of that little exercise was to test you on several fronts, see if any cream rose to the top," he said as his eyes sparkled. "And I must say that young Tatiana here was very impressive. Her instincts were to end a threat, and she reacted quickly and decisively. She knew what needed to be done the moment the gun flew out of my hand. And that's exactly why she's here. It's why all of you are here. But instead of ending threats, you're here to create them. You're here because your country needs you."

The general pulled his gloves taut as he stared out across the room.

"I think that's enough of an introduction for now," he said. "You may eat."

Tatiana stared at the plate in front of her.

She wondered if everyone else was as confused as she was. But for the moment, she didn't care. Her hunger overruled everything.

My country needs me?

CHAPTER 8

Washington, D.C.

BLACK NESTLED INTO the recliner in the safe house apartment assigned to Capt. Watkins. Knocking would've been more polite, but Black wasn't here to be polite. The more he learned, the more he believed the debacle in Russia was more than some personal vendetta by Col. Roman. Watkins knew more than he was telling, and Black was going to use one of his favorite approaches to find out what really happened.

Watkins's alarm squawked right at 6:30 a.m. Black heard the pilot slam his hand down, silencing the noise.

Thump, thump.

Black smiled.

Two feet on the floor. Even on his days off he can't escape the military rhythm.

The door creaked as it opened before Watkins stumbled into the living room. Black turned on the lamp next to him.

Watkins reacted quickly, training his gun on Black.

"What the hell?" Watkins said. "I almost shot you."

Black didn't move. "Do you always stumble into the kitchen with your weapon?"

"I do these days."

"You don't have anything to worry about from me."

"Then what are you doing here, sneaking into this safe house? You could've knocked."

Black chuckled. "Where would the fun have been in that?"

"Look, I know you spooks are—"

"I'm not a spook," Black said. "Not anymore, anyway. And I'm on your side, so stop treating me like the enemy."

"I'm not sure I know who to trust anymore."

Black stood and walked into the kitchen. "I'm squarely in your corner, Captain. If someone was trying to kill you, I want to know why before I address it. And your hunch that your base commander didn't like you for some reason doesn't cut it. There's more to the story that you're not telling me, isn't there?"

Watkins shook his head. "No, of course not. I told you everything."

"I don't think so. I've been doing this long enough to know when people are lying."

"So, you think I'm lying to you?"

Black shrugged. "Are you? If you aren't lying, you're omitting some very pertinent details, the kind of things I need to know to keep you safe and figure out what's really going. If you want me to help you, there can't be any secrets between us."

"I don't have any secrets."

"There's more to the story than you're telling me, isn't there?"

"Maybe."

"I can't protect you, much less help you, if you don't tell me what really happened over there in Japan. Base commanders don't just magically wake up one day and decide that they want to send one of their best pilots on a suicide mission."

Watkins eyed Black closely but didn't say anything.

"That's right," Black said. "I looked into your record. You're a model pilot, the kind the Air Force wants and needs. Yet you were thrust into an assignment that was designed to fail, designed to leave you for dead. At least that's what you're claiming."

"I'm not lying about that."

"I don't doubt that you are. But it's the *why* that interests me. You pissed off the wrong people, yet you've kept that information from me. I need the truth right now."

"You're on a fishing expedition, aren't you?" Watkins said.

"Look, I get it. You're scared. You're wondering if you can trust me. Well, I can promise you that I've had my share of run-ins with powerful people over the years. Some of them are behind bars, others are dead. And a few of them are still walking around thinking that they've gotten away with something. But they haven't. I just haven't finished the job yet. So, if you want to pretend like you're telling me everything, go ahead. You'll always live looking over your shoulder. But if you come clean now, I just *might* be able to help you."

Watkins furrowed his brow. "*Might* be able to?"

"I learned a long time ago not to make promises that I can't guarantee."

"I'm not sure that's good enough for me."

Black shrugged. "It'll have to be if you expect to have anyone in your corner, fighting corrupt behemoths in the American military."

Watkins sighed as he walked over to the window, staring out at the awakening bustle of the country's capital. "Just tell me what you want to know."

"How about let's start at the point in the story when you learned something you wished you hadn't?" Black said as he measured out coffee grinds.

"I'll never regret discovering what I did—as long

as something good comes out of it."

Black nestled the filter into the coffee maker before filling it with water and turning it on. "Let's hear it."

Watkins closed his eyes for a moment before he began. "About nine months ago, before a mission I was doing a routine inspection on my F-22 at Kadena Air Base when I noticed what appeared to be a couple of young teenage girls following one of the C-130 navigators around. Now, it's not completely unusual to see visitors on the base, particularly locals. But something about the way the girls were acting made me question whether they were actual guests."

"And like a good soldier, you couldn't just let it go, could you?" Black chimed in.

"Of course not. What would you do?"

"I'd check it out," Black said.

"Exactly," Watkins said. "Because I suspected that the navigator was doing something he shouldn't have, I hustled over near the hangar where his plane was, keeping a low profile. I waited a bit until I was sure no one was around and then entered through the cargo bay. There were several coffins inside, which made me wonder if I'd stumbled onto a morgue transport."

"A morgue transport?" Black asked.

Watkins nodded. "Yeah, you know, guys fighting

in the Middle East who get blown to bits by a roadside bomb or ambushed by some suicide bomber? They have to get home some way."

"And what'd you find?"

"A slew of coffins, but the funny thing is I hadn't heard of anyone getting killed," Watkins said. "Usually, it's all over base news and we have a moment of silence every Monday morning for the men killed in action. But it had been three months since I'd heard of a single soldier dying, much less a whole bunch of them. And based on the number of coffins, you would've thought we lost an entire platoon in Afghanistan."

"You hardly hear of any soldiers dying over there anymore."

"Precisely why I was skeptical," Watkins said, shaking his index finger. "I knew there was something shady going on. So, I snooped around. I was just about to open one of the coffins when the navigator caught me in the act. He asked me what I was doing and I had to think fast. I just told him that I was looking to see what kind of bed they'd put me in if I crashed and my body was recoverable. He just glared at me and asked me what I was really doing on the plane. I told him I was looking for one of my pilot buddies who flew C-130s. He said he wasn't scheduled to fly that day and that I should leave immediately. So I did, complying so I didn't make anyone suspicious."

"But apparently you did make someone suspicious, right?" Black asked.

Watkins nodded. "My theory is that the navigator told the base commander what I was doing. The next thing I know, I'm getting called onto the red carpet and getting reprimanded for my actions."

"And that's when you knew something was up," Black said.

"Absolutely right. I may have dropped it if I hadn't heard anything else about it. But when I was called in for something as inane as looking for a fellow pilot, I knew I'd stumbled onto something."

"You didn't consider the consequences?" Black asked.

"Of course I did," Watkins said. "But I don't want to be part of any organization that's transporting people illegally around the world."

The coffee maker sputtered as it spit out the final few drops. Black pulled out two mugs from the cupboard and filled them. "So, that's what you found?"

Watkins picked up one of the cups and took a sip. "Not right away. But I started snooping around on some of the manifests. The C-130s in Kadena were shipping somewhere in the neighborhood of thirty to forty coffins a week. A *week*! What the hell were we doing moving around that many boxes? That's when I knew something seriously shady was going on. But I needed to know what exactly before I could take it to any of my superiors, or even know which superiors to take it to."

"And that's when your base commander found out what you were doing?" Black asked.

Watkins nodded. "I got careless and was caught on the surveillance footage. One of the security guards turned me in to Col. Roman. He told me that what I was doing was endangering my career. At that point, I still didn't know exactly what was going on, but that only made me more curious. A week later, I hid up in the catwalk of one of the C-130 hangers. It was one of the ones assigned to that particular navigator who caught me the first time. I was pretty sure he was in on whatever was happening. So, I staked out that spot and waited."

"And what'd you find?" Black asked.

"Just as I suspected," Watkins said. "I watched the navigator sneak four young teenage girls onto the plane one night. I took a video of it and decided to show it to my squadron officer since I'd grown suspicious of Col. Roman being above board with everything."

Black nodded. "What did they do to make you fear for your life?"

"Col. Roman called me into his office and thanked me for alerting him to this issue. He said that he wanted to handle the discipline privately so it wouldn't become a public relations nightmare back home."

"And did he follow through with what he said?"

Watkins shrugged. "It seemed like it because the navigator was gone the next day. I asked around about him, and everyone said he was being reassigned."

"Yet you're still suspicious of Roman?"

"I'm getting there," Watkins said. "The day after I found out that navigator was being sent somewhere else, I get called into Roman's office. He tells me that he has a special reconnaissance assignment for me over Russia."

"You don't think your squadron officer is in on it?"

"He could be, but he's not the man pulling the strings," Watkins said. "The only one who could've assigned me to such a dangerous mission would've been Roman. And if nobody came looking for me after that, I can't help but draw any other conclusion. He has to be in on it, if not directing this entire illegal operation."

Black took a long sip of his drink as he considered what to say next. "Let's say you're right about all this. The biggest thing I need is proof. If I go up against these guys, I need to have irrefutable evidence that they're doing what you're claiming."

"I've got you covered," Watkins said. "I have a copy of the video I took of the navigator sneaking those girls onto a plane."

"How'd you manage that?"

"I uploaded it to a cloud server almost immediately after it happened," Watkins said. "And it's a good thing I did because when I got back here, all my personal effects were waiting for me. And the footage was deleted off my phone."

"That's definitely a red flag."

"I still don't know how they broke into my phone without my password."

Black's eyebrows shot upward. "You'd be amazed what tech geniuses can do."

"I've since made several copies and emailed friends the video as well, so killing me won't bury the truth."

"I'm gonna need a copy of all that so I can levy these charges," Black said.

Watkins held up his index finger as he drained the rest of his coffee. Then he marched back into his bedroom and returned dangling a small set of keys.

"What's this?" Black asked as he took them from Watkins.

"There's a locker at Union Station, number forty-two. You'll find reports detailing everything I told you along with a thumb drive containing the video. It'll contain all the evidence you'll need to make a compelling case to have Roman, the navigator, and whoever else is in on this scheme put in a dark hole somewhere for a very long time."

"Thanks," Black said. "I'll do what I can, and hopefully it'll be enough to protect you."

"Well, I'm planning on blowing the lid off this operation anyway at the ceremony today," Watkins said. "I don't think there'll be any way they can touch me after that."

"I wouldn't be so confident that they'll leave you alone," Black said. "Just because you expose them doesn't mean they can't find other creative ways to besmirch your good name and smear you with lies in public. If you plan on going through with that, I'm going to fight for you, but know that you'll be putting an even bigger target on your back."

Watkins nodded knowingly. "Thanks for believing me. I just want to see these bastards put away for what they're doing. It's disgusting. And violating the public's trust like this, using government funds and aircraft to transport these young girls around, it needs to be brought into the light and dealt with accordingly."

"I'm with you on that," Black said. "I'll see you

at the ceremony, and good luck."

"You too," Watkins said.

Black left the safe house and hustled to his car. He didn't have any time to lose if Watkins was going to make a public statement about what he saw in just a few hours.

CHAPTER 9

BLACK CHECKED THE TIME and considered if he could get to Union Station and back before the ceremony began. However, before he could make a final decision, his phone rang with a call from Blunt.

"You're up bright and early," Black said as he answered.

Blunt grunted. "Duty is always calling, even at this ungodly hour."

"I've been at the safe house talking with Watkins, so you're not rousing me from any sleep."

"Are you trying to outwork me?"

"Trust me. I don't want your job. But what I do want is to put away those men who tried to kill Watkins and cover it up."

"He somehow convinced you?" Blunt asked.

"It didn't take much, just the whole truth, which he'd withheld from us. And to be honest, I can't say I blame him."

"What happened over there?"

"He thinks his base commander is operating some kind of human trafficking ring."

"Human trafficking?"

"Yep," Black said. "And if you think about it, that's a far better way to transport people instead of in the cargo bay of a ship. Military planes go everywhere and aren't subject to the kind of inspections you get at an international shipyard. It's brilliant as far as illegal schemes go. If you've got a few crews willing to handle all the dirty work, it's nearly flawless."

"Unless someone catches you."

"And that's exactly what Watkins did. He stumbled on them moving a shipment of girls one day and reported it. He went back and filmed it for proof before getting his top secret assignment to spy on the Russians. Supposedly, there's a locker at Union Station that has all this documented."

"That certainly makes his fear sound more rational than when he debriefed with us in Morocco," Blunt said. "I'm always willing to give someone the benefit of the doubt, but he wasn't giving us much to go on."

"Can you blame him? I can't. The guy's scared for good reason. His superiors who he trusted tried to kill him and cover it up."

"Well, that makes my assignment for you today all the more important."

"You need me to do something for you?" Black asked.

"Yeah. Late last night, I met with Robert Besserman at the NSA, and he had a favor for me. He wanted me to have you check out the staging environment for Watkins's ceremony this morning."

"Why me?"

"There have been some threats levied against Senator Gaither that he wants us to do some due diligence on," Blunt said. "And since you'll already be there lending moral support to Watkins—and you're the best man for the job—I thought I'd give you something to do."

"Senator Gaither? Maybe I just won't show up."

Blunt chuckled. "I told Besserman something to that effect. He didn't think it was all that funny."

"I know it's our job to run these ops behind the scenes, but could you give me anyone to protect I despise more than Gaither?"

"I doubt it."

Black grunted. "So, what are the threats?"

"Maybe a deranged gunman? In the dossier Besserman prepared for me, they seem to think someone is going to shoot Gaither."

"That's a pretty specific threat. Anyone attempting to take Gaither out that way wouldn't be interested in keeping it a secret."

"They'd be a hero to more than half the country," Blunt said. "That guy's approval rating is just south of twenty percent, even from the people who voted for him."

"Those good Missourians cast a vote for him asking both parties to *show me another candidate*."

Blunt chuckled. "I can only imagine how bad the opposing party's candidate is for Gaither to keep getting elected."

"Maybe I'll be slack on my job today," Black cracked.

"Just keep your eyes peeled. Remember that we don't want anything happening to Watkins either."

"Roger that," Black said. "Don't tell Besserman this, but Watkins is top priority. The world needs men like him. And we sure can do without a few less blowhard politicians."

"You won't get any argument from me there. Just get out there early and do a preliminary threat assessment of the area. Send me what you come up with, and I'll forward it along to Besserman so he knows that we're taking this seriously. And then after that, keep an eye on Watkins."

"You got it."

* * *

THE SITE FOR the ceremony was on the grassy quad at the national mall. Black immediately saw it as a nightmare when it came to determining what position an assassin might take up. There were rooftops on the left and right, albeit heavily secure government buildings, most of which belonged to the Smithsonian museums. There were plenty of places with restricted views that could be difficult to inspect.

Black scanned the area, and his first thought was that if his assignment was to kill someone on stage, he'd sneak onto the grounds before anyone else and stake out in the trees. And since the leaves had yet to fall, it was a potential location that Black decided had to be checked out.

One by one, he ruled out certain trees as he peered up into the branches. There were a couple more that he proceeded to investigate, though he wasn't sure if even the most skilled marksman could shoot through foliage and hit a target from this distance. When he finished, he flashed the CIA credentials he possessed for situations like this and asked the security personnel if he could take a moment on the stage to look around. Once permission was granted, Black climbed up the steps and pulled out a pair of binoculars from his bag to look around.

During his preliminary assessment, Black didn't see many unobstructed views from the surrounding buildings. However, there was one: the Museum of

Natural Science offered a clean shot from the rooftop. Black would've picked it had he been given such an assignment, though it would've been far more complicated if the assassination attempt was anticipated. Either way, that's the location that made the most sense.

Black checked his watch. The ceremony was set to begin in just under two hours. And while it wasn't a huge amount of time, it was enough for him to hammer out a brief report and issue it to Blunt so he could do with it as he saw fit. Black found the nearest park bench and typed out his thoughts before emailing them to Blunt.

While writing, Black overheard a man claiming to be a reporter for The Washington Post in a heated argument with the ceremony's public relations firm rep. The reporter stomped off, sulking over the fact that his request had obviously been denied.

Once Black was finished, he sneaked onto the top of the Museum of Natural Sciences building just to see the potential target area from that location. It only reaffirmed his suspicion that it was the best position to shoot from, if that was a serious threat to Gaither. But Black figured the Missouri senator was just emphasizing how important he was that someone might actually want to kill him.

Black meandered back down to the national mall.

He was convinced that anyone who attempted to take out Gaither from even the best perches would find great difficulty in succeeding. A car bomb or a random mugging would be far better ways to kill him than picking him off in front of an audience during a live broadcast on television. Unless, of course, that was the objective: to kill Gaither while the world was watching. It'd send an ominous message for sure, but Black maintained skepticism the more he pondered it.

* * *

AN HOUR LATER, a crowd gathered for the ceremony. Black decided to linger near the back and see if he noticed anything that raised suspicions. Since the event was being held in such an open public place, there wasn't a way to funnel spectators through a security checkpoint, but the place was crawling with Washington police, keeping a careful eye on attendees who took a seat or were milling around the area.

Christina Shields parked Firestorm's surveillance van just off the mall in a metered spot. She only climbed out of the vehicle to feed the machine and avoid drawing any scrutiny from the Washington Metro police.

"What do you see out there?" she asked.

"Nothing that worries me yet," Black said. "You?"

"Nobody even remotely in the category of

potential shooter. And let me tell you, there's always at least two or three who appear like they'd enjoy filling someone with several pounds of lead."

Black continued to mill around until about fifteen minutes before the event was scheduled to begin. He slipped behind the stage with his security badge and strode up to Watkins.

The captain eased away from his handler, stepping out of earshot from her.

"I'm glad you could make it," Watkins said.

"Of course," Black said. "Are you ready for the consequences of what you're about to do?"

"If they kill me before I have the opportunity to expose their criminal behavior, what's the point? I will have given my very life for nothing. But if I can at least expose them and restore dignity and honor to the Air Force, this all won't be in vain."

"So far, the coast is clear."

"That's today," Watkins said. "Tomorrow's a new day, fraught with its own danger, no doubt. At least the cowards will have nowhere to hide in about twenty minutes after I'm done speaking."

"Well, good luck," Black said. "For what it's worth, I think you're the real deal. I really admire you for what you're doing."

"Don't ascribe such platitudes to me just yet. Check with me in five years and I'll tell you if I thought it was worth it."

Black shrugged. "Trust me. It's always worth it to take down corrupt leaders."

"I hope you're right," Watkins said with a nod.

Watkins's handler called for him.

"Gotta run. Catch you later."

"I promise I won't be sitting in your chair in the dark," Black said as he winked.

"And to think I ever thought fighter pilots were crazy," Watkins said before he spun and walked toward the woman organizing the ceremony's order of events.

Black strode around the side of the stage and scanned the area again. There still weren't any red flags.

"What are you seeing out there?" Shields asked over the coms.

"Calm. Almost eerily calm."

"I'm with you on that. There should be at least one loony-looking fellow stalking around behind the crowd with an overstuffed backpack. But I'm not seeing anything like that either. Well, keep me posted if anything changes."

"Likewise," Black said.

He meandered near the back, veering toward a clearing left of the stage. Given the likely locations of a shooter, Black determined it to be the optimum position to take in the scene.

"The U.S. Air Force" song blared over the speakers, garnering everyone's attention and kicking off the festivities. A ceremony emcee welcomed the crowd gathered at the mall, which Black estimated to be around three thousand people. It was a little smaller than he expected, but more than the number of chairs arranged on the lawn.

Black surveyed the attendees and still didn't see anything of note. "How are things looking on your end?"

"No nut jobs yet, though are you really gonna be inclined to stop something if Gaither takes a bullet?"

"It wouldn't be the worst thing to happen to Congress if he took an early retirement."

Shields chuckled. "That's about the best euphemism I've heard for one of our assignments in a long time."

"I'll be here all week," Black cracked.

The emcee continued the ceremony by inviting Senator Gaither onto stage. "This man needs no introduction as he's been a powerhouse in Washington from the day he arrived. Please put your hands together as we welcome Senator Todd Gaither."

"Powerhouse?" Shields said. "More like lightning rod or the congressional equivalent of a radio shock jock. He'll do anything to get a rise out of people."

"I don't know," Black said. "Shock jocks are

intentional about it, taking up a radical contrarian point of view for the purpose of getting big ratings. Gaither just does it every time he opens his mouth."

"Maybe he likes the limelight," Shields said.

"That's possible, but it's also sad since the bulb in that brain of his is so dull I doubt it could light up a closet."

Shields laughed again. "You're mighty witty today, Black. Did you have a little Bailey's with your coffee?"

"I can assure you that these one-liners are being conceived while completely sober."

Gaither stepped up to the lectern and glanced down at the notes in front of him. "Thank you. Thank you for taking time out of your busy schedules to brave Washington traffic and celebrate one hell of an American hero, Captain Trevor Watkins."

The crowd roared its approval with applause and whistling. Once the noise died down, Gaither continued.

"Capt. Watkins deserves a welcome like this, too. He was shot down in the service of his country and endured hardship while in a Russian gulag, slaving away and working tirelessly, all subject to the whims of overbearing taskmasters who didn't grant him even an ounce of respect."

"A gulag?" Shields whispered. "Is he just making this stuff up?"

"Sounds like it," Black said.

"Any potential hostiles out there yet?"

"Nope. All is still quiet, while the loudmouth continues to foist lies on the American people."

"Well, what did you expect?" Shields asked. "He is a politician. Aren't lies and embellishments what they do better than anything?"

"I wish you weren't right."

Gaither continued with his introduction before inviting Watkins to the stage. The crowd broke out into applause again as he plodded up the steps and strode toward Gaither. Overhead, a drone buzzed about twenty feet off the ground, capturing images of the event. The press corps photographers rushed closer to the stage in anticipation of the moment the two men met.

Black scanned the crowd again before searching on the nearby rooftops. Everything appeared above board. Out of the corner of his eye, he could see Gaither extend his hand to Watkins as the two drew near.

Then Gaither collapsed on stage, followed by Watkins a split second later. The two gunshots sent the crowd fleeing in chaos. Black glanced at the two men on stage as they were attended to by security personnel. He switched his focus to the ground to see if anyone was admiring his work or looking on with great satisfaction.

"Where did that come from?" Shields asked over the coms.

"I don't have a clue," Black said. "It was clear down here and on the rooftops. I didn't see anybody who could've made the shot."

Black stared at the scene, unable to do anything but try to assess how someone was able to kill both of those men. Gaither was the one who claimed to have credible threats against him and ask for more security. But Black could tell this was a pre-planned assassination attempt, one designed to throw off any investigation into the possibility that Watkins was the target.

Sirens wailed in the background as remaining law enforcement cleared out the lingering crowd. Black flashed his credentials to a police officer who ran by in an effort to avoid being hassled. After a few minutes, only a couple of rebellious photographers remained in a two hundred meter radius of the stage aside from the officials and paramedics who had just arrived.

"How bad is it?" Shields asked.

"I can't tell," Black said, "but I don't think it's good."

"Get closer and find out."

Black ventured up to the foot of the stage where medics were working furiously on Watkins, pumping his chest and trying to find a pulse. After a couple minutes, one of the men sighed and shook his head.

"He's gone," the man declared as his partner cursed.

Meanwhile, Gaither sat up, alert and somber, his bicep wrapped with a blanket draped over his shoulders.

"Is the senator all right?" Black asked a nearby attending paramedic.

The man looked at Black and nodded. "He was lucky. That was a clean shot that went straight through his bicep. If it had been over a few more inches, it would've exploded into his chest."

Black left the area and called Blunt.

"Did you hear the news?" Black asked as his boss answered.

"Shots fired at the ceremony," Blunt said. "Is Watkins gonna make it?"

"He's already gone," Black said.

"And Gaither?"

"He'll be just fine, according to one of the paramedics I spoke with. The bullet went clean through his bicep."

"This was a pro hit, designed to make it look like Gaither was the target."

"Exactly what I was thinking. So, what do we do now?"

Blunt grunted. "We're gonna blow the lid off this corruption and make sure Watkins didn't give his life in vain."

"I'm all in," Black said. "Just tell me where you want me to start."

"Go to Union Station and get all the proof Watkins collected," Blunt said. "I want to see all this information for myself before we decide to tangle with the people behind this."

"I'll call you when I have it."

CHAPTER 10

Two weeks earlier

TATIANA COULD HARDLY stand the stench after being locked in the shipping container for nearly two weeks. A toxic combination of body odor, urine, and stale air had settled over the entire steel box. Before she was thrust inside the eight-by-twenty-foot space, she'd never met the other eleven girls who joined her. With dim lighting, putrid conditions, and a mix of ethnicities, she didn't bother with attempting conversation. And she wasn't even sure what she'd talk about anyway if she could communicate. None of them wanted to be here, likely all wishing to be safe at home instead of tossed about at sea in a virtual prison.

The general had done his best to convince all of his so-called recruits that their sacrifice would be vital to the future of their country. But it was difficult for Tatiana to envision that at the moment. For the past two years, she went to bed each night exhausted from all of the work the general and his other instructors put her through. During that time, she grew stronger and more focused, earning her an early assignment.

She strode around the container, trying to ignore the smell as well as her cellmates. After a few minutes of pacing about, one of the girls stopped her and spoke in Russian. It was the first time anyone had said anything outside of a few things some of the girls mumbled in their sleep.

"It's not so bad," the girl said, her eyes betraying her statement.

Tatiana glared at the girl. "Get out of my way."

She didn't move. "You get used to it after a while."

"Get used to what?"

"The job. It could be worse. At least, that's how most of us feel. We could be at home getting beaten every night, wondering where our next meal will come from. At least we know we don't have to go back there, starving as we slip into bed, praying that we're still alive when morning comes—or perhaps praying for mercy that we won't."

Tatiana ignored the girl. "If you don't get out of my way, you'll regret it."

"It will get better."

Tatiana slammed the girl into the wall. She slid to the ground with a thud and then a whimper as

Tatiana continued pacing.

I'm not like any of you. I'm not even here for the same reason you are.

"Maybe next time you'll move," Tatiana said with a sneer.

The general had apologized as he bid Tatiana good luck. He explained how he would've preferred to fly her to the destination, albeit in a much more uncomfortable manner. The travel time would've been hours as opposed to weeks. But recent developments had dictated that she enter through a less scrutinized portal.

Being caged up for nearly two years made her less amicable than she was before she chased down that soccer ball in Bali. And spending a fortnight in such tight quarters shortened her fuse considerably.

Tatiana staggered as the ship swung around. Regaining her balance, she braced herself against the wall and realized they were finally docking at port.

* * *

TWO HOURS PASSED before Tatiana sensed any further movement. Outside the doors, she could hear workers chattering. Then with a sudden jolt, her steel box jerked upward. Tatiana had grown up near a shipyard and understood what was happening. Once ships were secured in the dock, cranes lifted the containers off the ship and moved them to solid ground where they were unloaded. The General had warned her that it would likely be several hours before anyone released her.

He was wrong. According to her watch, nearly twelve hours passed before someone unlocked the door. It swung open with a creak and clanked hard against the side.

Tatiana shielded her eyes as the beam from a powerful flashlight poured inside. A man waved it around the room before speaking.

"They're all here, alive and accounted for," he shouted over his shoulder.

"Bring 'em out," another man said.

Men rushed into the container and grabbed the girls, removing them one-by-one and placing them into a van. Tatiana ripped her arm away when they grabbed her, but to no avail. They dug their fingers into her skin, keeping her firmly in their grasp.

"It's okay, little girl," one of the men said in a gruff voice. "We're not going to hurt you."

Tatiana sneered at him before stopping just short of the van. The men released her and waited for her to get inside. When she didn't react fast enough, one of the men shoved her in the back, forcing her into the vehicle.

"It'll be better for you to follow directions immediately," he said.

Tatiana eased into her seat and stared blankly out the front window.

"Do you speak English?" he asked.

She didn't flinch.

The man reverted to Russian. "It'll be better for you to follow directions immediately."

Tatiana remained stoic, determining not to give the man even the slightest bit of pleasure that he guessed her country of origin.

Instead of ignoring her, he grabbed her face with his hand and forced her to look at him. "When I speak to you, you better acknowledge what I said. Is that clear?"

Tatiana mustered a feeble nod.

He shoved her head and spun back to retrieve the rest of the girls in the container. When they were all loaded into the two vans lined up by the door, they were driven to a dilapidated hotel only a few miles away.

They were led upstairs to their rooms with a pair of queen beds, four girls in each one. A sequin dress for each girl was hung in the closet.

"Shower and get dressed," the man said as he escorted Tatiana to her room. "We will be back in one hour to pick you up."

One of the girls in Tatiana's room turned on the television. The menu scrolled past with the date remaining in the upper right corner. Tatiana sighed as she glanced at it. It was her fifteenth birthday, and no one knew it.

She thought about her mother and the kind of fuss she used to make over each birthday. There were parties with friends, special mother-daughter adventures, or a lavish spending spree at her favorite fashion shop. But not today. There were no candles, no presents, no friends.

"Hurry up," the man barked as he knocked on the door.

When Tatiana stepped out of the shower, she shimmied her way into the tight, silver sequin dress that was the closest to her size. She was still combing her hair when a harsh knock at the door startled her.

"Let's go, ladies," the man said. "It's time to get to work."

CHAPTER 11

Great Falls, Virginia

BLUNT STOPPED AT THE gatehouse and showed his driver's license to the guard stationed there. After carefully studying the ID, he dialed a number and had a brief conversation before waving Blunt through. Blunt found gated communities to be contentious, but he understood the desire for privacy by some people, especially the head of the NSA.

Blunt lumbered up the steps to Robert Besserman's house and rang the doorbell. When he didn't answer, Blunt walked around the side of the spacious yard and found Besserman relaxing in a chair by a dormant fire pit, his eyes closed with a drink in his hand. The sun was setting just over the Potomac River, a scenic view that the NSA director enjoyed each day after work, if he was awake to see it.

"If you don't open your eyes, you're going to miss that," Blunt said, gesturing toward the sunset.

Besserman bolted upright in his seat. "J.D., what the hell are you doing here? You're interrupting my after-work moment of zen."

"We need to talk, Bobby. And as much as I trust *you*, I didn't want to risk someone eavesdropping on our conversation in any form or fashion."

"And you think my home is safer?"

"I'd hope so. You are the head of the NSA, after all."

A wry grin spread across Besserman's face. "Of course my house is safe. I just don't really consider this the best place to discuss national security implications."

"Sorry to spring this on you," Blunt said, "but I'm just leery of everybody these days."

"Let's go inside," Besserman said. "I'll fix you a drink."

After ushering Blunt into the house, Besserman headed straight for the bar. "I've got some great scotch here."

"It's not one of those conversations, Bobby. I want to keep this brief because we've got work to do."

Besserman stopped and eyed Blunt closely. "What is it?"

"What did you think of the fiasco at the National Mall earlier today?" Blunt asked.

"I thought your people were there to ensure

something like that didn't happen."

Blunt shook his head. "It didn't matter, because someone wanted Watkins dead."

"You think Gaither wasn't the target?"

"That's what we're trying to figure out, but I think this whole Gaither death threat thing was a smoke screen."

"By who? Gaither or the shooter?"

Blunt shrugged. "That's what we're trying to figure out. All I know is that in this business when something seems coincidental, it usually isn't."

"Don't forget that the president was supposed to host this ceremony in the Rose Garden, so if you're suggesting that this was coordinated, there has to be some high-level officials involved."

"Or at least capable of pulling some strings to manipulate the situation."

Blunt took a seat on the couch.

"Maybe this is one of those conversations," Besserman said as he settled into the chair across from Blunt. "You sure you don't want a drink?"

Blunt waved his hand, rejecting Besserman's offer again. "The timing of everything is what makes me suspicious. The only good fortune we've received here is that me and my team know about all the moving parts involved here—the truth behind the Watkins situation, the death threats on Gaither's life, the shifting venue for the welcome home ceremony. And it sure does seem that the ordeal surrounding Gaither was designed to make everyone think he was the intended target."

"Well, I'm inclined to agree with you on this one," Besserman said, "especially after what I found today."

"*You* found? Are you doing your own sleuthing these days?"

"My trust level on this investigation isn't very high. I'm just as suspicious of Gaither as you are, but I wanted to find out why you thought so before revealing this." Besserman leaned forward and nudged a manila folder across the coffee table toward Blunt.

"What's this?" Blunt asked as he picked up the documents.

"Gaither's phone records, including several of those voice messages supposedly left for him."

"And what did you find?"

"Gaither played the death threats for us from his phone, reluctant to give it to us since he conducts so much business with it. So, I simply asked him when he received those messages. I accessed his voicemails remotely and then got a copy of his phone records. I tried to see who made the calls, but I could only trace them back to a burner phone."

"That wouldn't be surprising in either case,"

Blunt said as he scanned the numbers.

"Exactly," Besserman said, pointing his index finger at Blunt. "But I went back through the numbers and found that whoever left this message was also the same person who Gaither called back later that night and spoke with on the phone for nearly fifteen minutes."

"Nice work," Blunt said. "This gives us something to go on."

"Oh, no. It's more than that. Playing a hunch, I took it a step further and triangulated the position of several of his staffers' phones around that same time to see if any of them were in the area. Turns out one of them was."

Blunt's eyebrows shot upward. "You got a name?"

"Mark Baldwin," Besserman said. "He's been one of Gaither's longtime staffers."

"What are you thinking? Baldwin is carrying out orders from someone else? Or do you think he's doing Gaither's bidding?"

Besserman grinned. "That's what I want you to find out for me. I can only do so much."

"And you think we'll be able to levy charges against Gaither?"

"That depends."

"On what?" Blunt asked.

"Everything hinges on your team's ability to get to the truth on this one. Not that I wouldn't mind putting Gaither away, but if he's just a pawn, we need to use him as bait to catch who's really behind this kind of mayhem. I don't want to play whack-a-mole on this one."

"Got it," Blunt said. "Cut off the head of the snake."

Besserman stood and gestured toward the door. "You're right. This wasn't one of those conversations. You need to get moving because you've got a lot of work to do."

Blunt shook Besserman's hand, but the NSA director called Blunt's name before he could make it to his car.

"Yeah?"

"Next time, I want you to try this scotch I have."

"Next time, Bobby. Next time."

Blunt climbed into his car and then scanned the area as he pushed the ignition button. He was firmly convinced that Watkins wasn't paranoid after all. Now Blunt just had to convince the people that mattered— or else handle the situation some other way.

CHAPTER 12

Washington, D.C.

BLACK ZIPPED UP HIS JACKET and pulled it taut as he strode into Union Station, a backpack hanging off his left shoulder. With a quick glance, he checked to make sure he wasn't being followed. Determining that no one was watching him, he pressed ahead, navigating through the congested passageway. While many commuters continued about their day in a business-as-usual mode, Black noticed the heightened security and the nervous looks worn on the faces of most people.

When Black reached the lockers, he retrieved the key from his pocket. The moment felt somewhat haunting, especially remembering Watkins' comment the moment he placed the keyring in Black's hands.

I'm planning on blowing the lid off this operation later today.

Watkins never got the chance, but Black wasn't

going to let the pilot's sacrifice be for naught. Black felt confident he could use the information Watkins left to get justice for him and perhaps hundreds of others.

Upon descending into the bowels of the building, Black worked his way through a quiet maze of lockers and found No. 42. He took one more quick look around before opening it. Inside, he found a folder containing grainy screenshots, obviously taken from the footage he recorded. There were also several pages of notes about the operation and descriptions of the more than two dozen girls he observed being led into the C-130 cargo hold at Kadena Air Base. Black snapped the folder shut and tucked it into his backpack. He re-secured the lock and then headed toward the exit.

As Black turned the corner, he was greeted with a solid punch to his stomach. He staggered backward in pain, slamming into the lockers and using them to remain upright. By the time he looked up, his attacker, clad in dark clothes with a ski mask, was in the middle of swinging his nightstick at Black's head. Black ducked down and took advantage of the man's imbalance. Black struck his first counterblow, jamming his foot upward into the man's crotch. The force of the kick sent him airborne before he crashed into the lockers behind him.

Black scrambled to his feet and darted toward the door. But the combatant managed to get a solid grip on Black's bag and yanked him down. Black clutched the strap with both hands, refusing to let go at the expense of breaking his fall. He skidded across the floor, coming to a stop against the far wall. When he did, his hands jarred loose. And the attacker was right there to seize the bag.

Black fought hard, spinning around on his back to sweep the man's legs out from underneath him. The pack flew a few meters away, leading to a mad dash for it. Black crawled to it first and secured it before ramming his foot into the man's face. He groaned in pain, but Black didn't let up, following with two more shots to the man's jaw. Sensing an opportunity to knock the man out and get some answers, Black hustled to his feet again only to turn around and watch the man race out of the room. Across the way, he heard the door slam shut, but Black remained skeptical that he was alone.

Black crept quietly through the maze of lockers until he reached the doorway. He opened the door swiftly to mitigate a surprise attack and saw no one around him. With the area relatively clear, Black headed up the steps and returned to his car. He turned the key in the ignition as the engine roared to life.

He dialed Shields's number and put her on

speaker phone as he drove out of the parking garage.

"Are you at the office?" Black asked.

"I am now. I just got back from the dealership picking up my rental for the week."

"Car trouble?"

"I need a new alternator," she said. "Fun times. Did you need something?"

"Maybe an aspirin for this headache I've got," Black said. "Someone just tried to kill me."

"Were you trying to get that proof Watkins left you?"

"Yep. Someone ambushed me as I was leaving."

"Do you still have the files and footage?"

Black sighed. "No concern about how I'm doing? No questions about my health?"

"I know you're alive since you're talking to me," she said. "So don't be such a drama queen. I can dress your little owwies later."

"The lack of empathy you have is shocking sometimes," Black cracked.

"And your lack of toughness makes me wonder how you ever thought this would be a profession you would enjoy. I have half a leg missing, but you don't hear me complaining about that, do you? You try to milk these encounters for all they're worth. You probably don't even have a shiner."

"How many times do I have to tell you that hits

to the face are far less effective than a throat punch? The pros know where to hit."

"So this guy was a pro?" Shields asked.

"No doubt about it."

"I hope this call wasn't simply to gain sympathy from me."

Black chuckled. "Of course not. I know better by now. I've worked with you for two years now. I know what to expect, but I was hoping you would at least show some concern."

"What do you need?"

"Can you get access to the security footage from Union Station for about the last half hour?" Black asked. "I want to see if we can track this guy and figure out who he is."

"I'll see what I can do," she said. "You think this is the same guy who shot Watkins?"

"This thug was more of a bruiser than a sniper. I'm thinking more of a frontlines guy. But I don't know."

"All right, I'll get to work on that."

"And I'm going to upload everything I got from Watkins right now so that you'll have it in case this guy makes another run at me."

"I'll be on the lookout for it," Shields said. "And I'll keep you posted on what I find."

Black hung up and adjusted his rearview mirror

so he could see if the attacker did manage a facial bruise.

"Nothing," Black said aloud as he stroked his chin and smiled. "Still handsome as ever."

He heard a cackling noise and glanced around his car to determine the source of the laughing.

"Hello," he said as he picked up his cell phone.

"I'm still here," Shields said. "You forgot to hang up, and I'm too busy to do it myself."

"Laugh it up," Black said. "You can act like it's funny that I was talking to myself, but everybody does it."

"Maybe, but you won't ever catch me telling myself that I'm *as beautiful as ever*," she said before breaking into another chuckle. "I only wish I had accompanying video, but I'm sure it would be disappointing compared to how I imagined that little exchange with yourself and the mirror."

"I'm hanging up now, this time for real," Black said.

Black pulled out his laptop and transmitted all the files to Shields. After he finished, he headed toward the office. There was still plenty of digging to be done if he and Shields were going to expose who was behind Watkins's death and the conspiracy he uncovered.

CHAPTER 13

TATIANA RAN HER FINGERS along the contours of her body, sliding the sequins on her dress in the same direction. She crossed her legs as she took a seat on the foot of the bed in an upstairs room at an extravagant house overlooking the water. This was the moment she had been waiting and training for. After being away from her family and under the general's tutelage for the past two years, she was ready to prove herself.

Before Tatiana left for the United States, the general had promised her that all she needed to do was complete her assignment and he would allow her to go back home to her family. That's all she wanted, to go back home and be normal again. However, she wasn't sure that was even possible. The time she'd spent preparing to serve her country had changed her in more ways than one. Dreams of playing soccer had long since died. And she didn't think she'd ever see the world the same again.

The general had made quite an impact with his theatrical stunts the first day of the incoming class of recruits. But it didn't take long before she started witnessing events that weren't staged moments designed to put fear in all the trainees. He was demanding—and ruthless when his standards weren't met. Daily he emphasized the importance of precision and how attention to detail could mean the difference between survival and failure. And there were no acceptable alternatives other than success.

Tatiana could almost hear his voice in her head as she sat on the end of the bed and waited.

"Tatiana, you're one of our brightest. You will be hailed as a hero and forever etched into the lore of your country if you pay heed to what I'm saying and learn to apply it."

A knock at the door made her jump, even though she was anticipating it.

"Come in," she said before forcing a smile.

A man dressed in a light-gray suit with a black tie strode inside. He spoke in a Russian accent and barely looked her in the eyes. "Are you ready?"

Tatiana exhaled slowly. "I think so."

"Think so or know so?" he asked as he knelt next to her at the foot of the bed. "Because there is a big difference, you know."

"Think," Tatiana said, setting her jaw. "I've never done this before, so you should know as well as anyone that your first time makes you nervous, even if you are confident you know exactly what to do."

"Just don't think about it," he said. "That's the easiest way. It'll be over before you know it. And I'll come in and help you when it's over."

"Send him in," she said.

With that, the man exited the room. She waited patiently, visualizing everything she was about to do. The longer she waited, the more she felt physically ill. There was only one thing that kept her calm enough to follow through with her assignment.

It's all for my country.

She heard the approaching footsteps before they halted just outside her door. When the person finally knocked, she swallowed hard and slipped her hand inside her purse.

"Come in," she said.

The man who strode into the room looked vaguely familiar, though she couldn't place him. He shut the door behind him without ever taking his eyes off Tatiana. He looked her up and down before easing onto the bed next to her.

"My God," he said, "how do they make Russian women so beautiful?"

Tatiana wrapped her fingers around the dagger inside her purse. "I don't know. Why don't you ask him yourself?"

With that, she whipped out the blade and jammed it into the man's throat. She backed away as he flopped around on the floor, trying to stop the bleeding. But it was of no use. She had severed his carotid artery. In less than fifteen seconds, he'd passed out from the sudden decrease in blood pressure. In just under sixty seconds, he was dead.

She wanted to scream as she stepped back and realized what she'd done. She resisted the tears that welled up in her eyes.

All for my country.

The man in the suit rushed into the room and directed her to avoid touching the body.

"Step over him," the man said. "He's not going to hurt you now."

Tatiana looked away as he held out his hand and assisted her. He guided her to the exit and told her to wait in the hallway.

He returned shortly with a plastic bag containing one of the man's fingers. He handed it to her along with a pair of gloves.

"This is what I need?" she asked.

"You need his fingerprint to access the files. Once you have access, place this back in the bag, do whatever you need to do to get the files the general requested, and then return the body part to me."

Tatiana nodded and followed the man's instructions. In a matter of minutes, she was rummaging around on the dead guy's computer, downloading files from a particular folder onto a flash drive. When she finished, she wiped down the computer and took the finger and the data files to the man in the suit.

"Will I be able to go home now?" she asked.

The man took the items from her and stared at her, eyeing her cautiously as if he wasn't sure if she was serious.

"You're kidding, right?" he asked.

"No, I'm not. Can I go home now?" she asked, her lips quivering as she waited for his response.

"I'm afraid not. You don't go home until the general says he's done with you."

"So what do I do now?"

The man reached inside his jacket pocket and produced an envelope along with a cell phone. "Your instructions are in there along with all the documents you'll need."

She huffed as she accepted them. "What if I just—"

"Don't even think about leaving," the man said. "He knows how to find everyone. And don't think you'll be the exception. People who stiff him learn the hard way. You're beautiful and have your whole life ahead of you. I'd hate for you to make such a mistake this early in life."

Tatiana nodded and walked downstairs, opening the envelope as she did. She glanced at the orders, which she was instructed to memorize before destroying. Not wanting to take any chances, Tatiana utilized her training, committing everything on the directive to memory before lighting the paper on fire.

She didn't like the general's bait and switch tactic, but she determined to endure it.

For country.

CHAPTER 14

Washington, D.C.

BLACK PUT ON A pot of coffee per Shields's request as they continued to follow all the threads that were dangling from Watkins's documented proof. However, it was more like circumstantial evidence. There was no doubt something illicit was going on, but determining the players involved wasn't easy. Shields pointed out how many of the communications were in code, not to mention that the email addresses were free accounts that were easy to hack but difficult to trace back to the original sender, much less prove it in a court of law.

"Can't you use IP addresses to track these people?" Black asked.

"Sure, but if you're even remotely savvy on computers, you can spoof your IP address, making it next to impossible to know where an email originated or was sent to. But there are some ways to get around that; it just takes more time. Hence, the pot of liquid caffeine brewing in the kitchen."

The Firestorm offices were located in the basement of one of the tallest buildings in Washington. Black always thought it was a shame that when he did have to go to discuss matters in person or engage in a more in-depth investigation, he only had walls to look at instead of some scenic view. He told Blunt on more than one occasion that being a tenant in that building was the worst idea for team morale, even if there were only two people working out of that particular Firestorm office. And while Black hadn't met anyone else affiliated with Firestorm other than Blunt and Shields, there were supposedly two other teams assisting Blunt with his secret missions, housed in other spots.

"I bet the other Firestorm team has a better view than this," Black said as he delivered a mug of piping hot Colombian dark roast coffee to Shields.

"You know when I work, I don't have time to stare out a window because I'm looking at my screen, trying to get stuff done," Shields said. "You should try it sometime. It might make you forget that we're stuck in this hole in the ground."

"See," Black said, snapping and then pointing his finger at Shields, "you don't like it either, do you?"

"No, but I don't moan about it either," she said

before taking a big swig of her drink. "Now get over here and help me. We've got work to do if we're going to catch these bastards."

Black scooted a chair next to Shields.

"You're on my foot, you know," she said.

"Oh, I'm so sorry. I didn't mean to—"

"My prosthetic," she said. "Do I look like I'm in pain? But if you don't take your chair off my leg, I'm going to take it off and hit you with it."

"Look, I didn't mean anything. I just—"

"Oh, cut it out, Black," she said. "I'm just messing with you. Now will you read off these numbers to me so this process can go faster?"

Black read off a series of numbers, which Shields keyed into her computer at a furious rate.

"What are we doing again?" Black asked.

"We're trying to figure out where in the world these email addresses are that Col. Roman was sending messages to."

"I thought you said that couldn't be done."

Shields clucked her tongue. "I said it could be done but it just takes more time." She held up her mug. "Remember?"

"I feel like my talents are being wasted here," Black said dryly.

"I'm sorry that there aren't any heads to crack or villains to fill with lead. Sometimes the unsexy side of espionage is found in the mundane tasks. Don't worry, I'll let you out of this cage soon enough so you can go get us a paddy wagon full of these assholes."

For the next half hour, Black read off numbers to Shields. The rote work annoyed Black, but he was willing to do whatever it took to catch the people who rubbed out Watkins.

After Shields entered one of the long strings of digits, she hit enter and then pumped her fist.

"What is it?" Black asked.

"I've got something. This particular receiver didn't mask his IP address."

Black leaned forward, peering at the monitor. "Who does it belong to?"

"Let me enter this into my database over here and see what I come up with," she said.

"What database is that?"

"It's my highly secret one, the one that is affiliated with a list of both friends and foes in our military as well as most foreign militaries," she said, talking more quickly as she went. "It's like a world directory of IP addresses from computers that our good friends over at the NSA have hacked over the years."

Black sipped his drink as he watched the progress bar crawl toward one hundred percent. He waited anxiously without saying a word.

"You know what's crazy?" Shields said. "Roman wrote to this particular address several times, and this one time the IP address wasn't blocked. This is the kind of stroke of luck we need to get a breakthrough here and figure out who all is involved in this."

"I'm betting it's someone in our own military," Black said. "I wouldn't mind cracking a few heads belonging to some crooked armed forces generals."

"I don't doubt that. But let's temper that response until we actually know what's—" She stopped, her mouth falling agape.

"What is it?" Black asked. "Or maybe I should say: *who* is it?"

"Go get Blunt," she said. "He's going to want to hear this."

Black hustled down the hall and motioned for Blunt to join.

"What is it?" Blunt asked.

"Shields has something."

"What does she have?"

Black shrugged. "I don't know. She won't tell me. I'm just following orders here. She said to come down here and get you."

Blunt grunted as he stood and meandered after Black down the short corridor to Shields's workspace. "Is this gonna make my day?"

"It'll make your year, maybe," she said. "But

we've figured out at least one person who Roman was communicating with."

"Who?" Blunt asked.

"Ivan Kozlov, the Russian military commander running the installment on Kamchatka where Watkins was detained," Shields said with a smile.

"Kozlov?" Blunt asked, furrowing his brow.

She nodded. "The one and only."

"What do you know about him?" Black asked.

"Just that he's about as bad as any terrorist you'll ever come across," Blunt said. "He has no conscience, but he's also subject to the whims of General Volkov, who is much more measured in how he makes his decisions."

"I guess this email might make more sense in light of that background," Shields said.

"What did it say?" Blunt asked.

"I found this email that Roman sent to Kozlov discussing the specifics of a drop. And I'm hoping that doesn't mean that the two are exchanging military secrets."

Blunt shrugged. "It's hard to say. I looked at Roman's file. Everything in it screams *patriot*, but his personality evaluation describes him as, and I quote, opportunistic."

"So maybe he's just taking advantage of an opportunity to build a fat little nest egg on the side without selling out his country?" Shields asked.

"That's possible, but I don't know anyone in his right mind who would trust Kozlov, especially if you're claiming to be a flag-waving, red-white-and-blue wearing American. Kozlov is a snake if there ever was one."

"Where does that leave us?" Black asked.

"From everything I'm reading, it simply appears as though Kozlov and Roman have developed some type of partnership to transport girls around the world," Blunt said.

"Kozlov supplies the girls, and Roman simply provides the means to get them wherever they need to be," Shields said.

Blunt grunted. "A regular FedEx for human trafficking slaves—and collaborating with the Russians to do it."

"We need to go after him right away," Black said. "Who knows how many secrets have been compromised already by this kind of reckless behavior."

"Not yet," Blunt said. "If we go right for the jugular, we might end up missing the key players behind this, and then the people truly responsible will get away without a single consequence."

"What do you propose we do about it then?" Black asked.

Blunt smiled and winked. "I say we set a trap."

CHAPTER 15

EARLY THE NEXT MORNING, Black sat in the waiting room of George Washington Hospital. In less than five minutes after arrived, he grew tired of the inane morning gameshow airing on the television affixed to the far wall. The only other person in the area was a man resting his head against the wall, a fedora covering his face. Black searched for a staff member who could change the channel with a remote control before deciding to do it himself. The only thing he could stand was the news, though he'd grown tired of the political bias shrouding itself in claims of objectivity.

Listening to one of the anchors blather on about the dire state of the current administration made him want to throw a chair through the TV. But instead, he got up and marched over to the television to change it again before the newscaster stopped and announced a breaking news report. Black froze and watched.

"Tech billionaire Jeff Carson died last night at his

twenty-seven million dollar mansion overlooking Half Moon Bay in what local authorities are calling one of the most shocking murders in recent memory. Carson made his fortune by helping create web-based security systems that enabled both homeowners and business owners the ability to monitor all their cameras with one of the most innovative apps available for smart phones. Carson leaves behind his estranged wife and movie star, Paris Nix, and a billion-dollar fortune."

The man in the corner removed the hat from his face. "Well, I'm not Colombo, but my money is on the wife."

"Did she have motive?" Black asked.

"I think she was broke."

"Broke? Paris Nix?"

"Yeah, she blew it all partying, and her last few movies bombed. I don't think she's been in a film in at least five years."

"Huh," Black said. "I need to get to the movies more often."

"No, you don't," the old man said. "You're not missing anything. Trust me."

Black chuckled. "Well, I guess we'll find out soon enough if you're right."

"We should know by tonight if the San Francisco PD have a collective IQ above 110."

Black smiled and shook his head as he looked at

the man. "Do you do stand-up?"

"Not without a walker," the man said, gesturing to the device to his right. "I'll be here all week, literally. I'm not going anywhere."

Black smiled, suppressing another laugh.

A nurse appeared from the hallway and made eye contact with Black. "Sir, the senator said he'll see you now."

"You take care," Black said to the old man.

Black followed the nurse down the hallway to Senator Gaither's room. A pair of FBI agents stood watch outside and exchanged a knowing nod with Black before he flashed his credentials and was permitted inside.

"Senator Gaither?" Black said as he closed the door.

"Yes?" Gaither said as he sat up.

"I'm Agent Ted Malone," Black said, holding up his phony CIA credentials. "The agency wanted me to talk with you about what happened."

Gaither leaned forward and squinted, trying to read the badge. "Isn't this FBI jurisdiction?"

"When one of our own legislators is attacked in broad daylight like you were, we all work together to catch the bastards. There's no territorial chest pumping on these kinds of cases. If we can pool our resources to reach a more expedient resolution, that's what we do."

"Sounds like a great plan to me," Gaither said. "Do you have leads yet?"

Black walked over to the lamp on the side of Gaither's bed and turned it on, fingers lingering beneath the shade for a beat. "Well, I wanted to ask you about the threats you received. Did those voices sound familiar?"

He shook his head. "I've had angry constituents call, ticked that I voted one way or another, screaming that they'll never vote for me again. But up until recently, I've never had anyone threaten to kill me."

"Did they specify why they were upset?"

Gaither sighed and looked out the window. "I suppose it had to do with some of the legislation I recently spearheaded. When you go against big business, you make a lot of people mad."

"Is this the bill you brought to the senate that eliminates local tax breaks for some of the massive conglomerates?"

"Yeah, that's the one. All those fat cats don't like realizing that their free ride is up. And when that happens, they send their people after you. Usually it's just a simple threat to steer voters in another direction. But this time, they seemed intent on taking things a little further."

"But that bill died last week, didn't it?"

"Believe it or not, the halls of congress aren't

exactly teeming with principled people. When it comes to members of congress and the senate, if there's a conflict between the representative's needs or desires and his or her district, I'll tell you which direction they end up voting ninety-five percent of the time—their own."

"I think that's common knowledge, sir," Black said.

Gaither huffed a soft laugh through his nose. "I'm afraid you're probably right. So, have you been able to pinpoint who the perpetrators might be?"

"We're working hard, but we are very thorough and won't just take everything at face value."

"And where has that gotten you so far?"

"Believe it or not, it's opened up plenty of possibilities, including the fact that you may not have been the intended target."

Gaither's jaw dropped as he narrowed his eyes. "Are you kidding me? Some nut threatens to kill me and then has the audacity to actually take a shot. But now you're telling me the agency thinks that maybe I wasn't the intended target?"

"You're still here, aren't you?"

"They missed," Gaither said. "Though not entirely."

"But you'll live," Black said. "Capt. Watkins, on the other hand, will have dirt shoveled over his body later this week. And the fact that he's dead doesn't surprise me."

Gaither furrowed his brow. "Oh? Why's that?"

"We had an intriguing debriefing with him last week after he returned from Russia. The information that guy gave us—amazing. When he walked out the door, I had a hunch he might find himself on the business end of a bullet. And that was just the tip of the iceberg. He was scheduled to speak further with the agency about what led to his ill-fated mission."

"Who do you think shot him?" Gaither asked.

"No clue at this point, but we're digging. And I can promise you that we're going to find whoever is responsible for his death."

"Of course you are," Gaither said. "That's the job, isn't it?"

"Yes, sir. All day, every day."

"Well, good luck. I hope you catch the bastard and put him away for life."

Black nodded. "I intend to, sir."

With that, Black spun and headed toward the door. He grabbed the knob and stopped, glancing over his shoulder at Gaither.

"Get well, sir. We need you back soon. The halls of congress need legislators like you who put their constituencies' needs over his own."

"I appreciate that, Agent Malone. And good luck.

I hope you catch the evil men who tried to have me killed."

"I won't let you down, Senator," Black said before he slipped into the hallway and shut the door behind him.

He hustled downstairs and waited until he reached the privacy of his car to call Blunt.

"How'd it go?" Blunt asked.

"The trap has been laid," Black said. "Time for phase two."

CHAPTER 16

BLACK RACED to the Firestorm offices, convinced that Senator Gaither would take the bait. But Black couldn't be too sure. Usually, his assignments consisted of eliminating someone as quietly as possible. However, this time he was involved in the espionage side of the operation on a far deeper level than normal. And he found that it gave him a rush.

He dialed Shields's number and then downshifted before stomping on the gas and weaving between a pair of slower moving vehicles on the Beltway. The engine in his Mercedes S560 whined before he jammed it into a higher gear. As he weaved in and out of traffic, he waited for Shields to answer.

"Is anything happening yet?" Black asked.

"You must be about the most impatient person I've ever met," she said before clucking her tongue. "I can't imagine how you deal with going to the DMV every year."

"I don't," Black said. "I pay the extra amount so

I only have to visit every four years. It's easier that way—on all of us."

"Are you an organ donor?"

"Currently? No. And if I die prematurely, I'm betting that my organs will be in no shape to be transplanted into anyone else's body. I'll either be slashed up or riddled with bullets, making my donor designation little more than an altruistic gesture."

"Your honesty is a breath of fresh air—and you're also driving me nuts."

Black chuckled. "Why? Because I expect results so quickly?"

"Yeah," she said. "That's not how things work when it comes to laying a trap. You have to bide your time and wait for the person to make a mistake."

"Not when you scare the hell out of someone like I just did."

"Did you threaten him?"

"Of course not," Black said. "I simply told him that the agency didn't think that he was the target from the attempted assassination."

"And how'd he respond to that?"

"Just like you would suspect: shock, awe, disbelief. The usual suspects."

Shields sighed. "And look where that got you."

"Actually, I can't see where that got me, which is why I'm calling you," Black said. "I was hoping that you could tell me what became of our stunt."

"Why? Because you wanted to know if your story put the fear of God in him?"

"Something like that," Black said.

"Unfortunately, he hasn't done a thing since you left," Shields said. "Right after you exited the room, one of the guards went in with a doctor and a couple of nurses. The doctor addressed Gaither directly and urged him to take some pills. Gaither refused, resulting in a tense standoff, which is still taking place as we speak."

"If anything changes, keep me posted."

"Roger that," Shields said before she hung up.

Black sped along the surface streets and pondered how any so-called public servant could lose his bearings so much that he drifted this far off course. Participating in a human trafficking ring to line your pockets seemed like a massive detour from helping people. To profit off the vulnerable and destroy their youth? The thought angered Black the more he considered the consequences of such an organized crime. The base commander certainly knew what he was doing. And Gaither was involved on some level, though to what extent is what Black wanted to know. Was it simply a stunt to gain public sympathy? Or was he a pawn used by his aides? Or was he actively participating in helping Roman ferry teenage girls around the world and reaping a windfall? If the latter was true, Gaither wouldn't wait long to reach out to Roman and warn him.

When Black pulled into the parking garage, he drove to the bottom level and entered the building through the secure access door.

"Tell me we've got something good," Black said as he pulled up a chair next to Shields.

"If your definition of *good* is footage of the senator snoring, I have it," she said. "Otherwise, I'm afraid you're going to be disappointed."

Black sighed and shook his head. "I so wanted that jerk to be involved so if anything I'd never have to hear from him again. His very voice is like fingernails on a chalkboard for me."

"And most Americans feel the same as you do," Shields said. "He's got an eighteen percent approval rating nationwide. *Eighteen percent!* Do you know how awful something has to be to earn a rating that low? Osama Bin Laden had at least twenty percent."

Black chuckled. "I think Brussels sprouts are at least twenty-five percent."

"They'd be at a hundred percent if people cooked like them like I do."

"What's your secret?

"Cheese and bacon," she said with a wink. "I could make a pile of dirt taste like a gourmet meal with enough cheese and bacon."

"I had no idea you were a chef," Black said.

"I know what you're doing here, and it won't work."

"What? I just made a statement."

"You're fishing for a dinner invite. But it's not gonna happen, so just forget about it."

Black sighed. "You show interest in a colleague's hobby and this is what happens."

Shields slapped Black with the back of her hand. "Look, Gaither's awake."

They both leaned closer to the monitor streaming the images from the senator's room. Gaither sat up and glanced around the room. He appeared to scan the ceiling, as if searching for something.

"What's he looking for?" Black asked.

"I don't know. Maybe he thinks there are security cameras in the ceiling."

After a few seconds, he leaned toward the bedstand on his right and snatched up his phone. He entered his passcode and started scrolling.

"It looks like he's texting," Black said. "Can you zoom in?"

"This is as close as we can get here," she said. "But I think you're right. There is something I can do to enhance this a bit on my other monitor."

Shields captured a still shot from one screen and

moved it to another before typing furiously on her keyboard.

"Is it working?" Black asked.

"Patience, patience," Shields said. "I'm almost there."

A few seconds later, Shields cropped in on the phone, which was held at just the right angle for the camera Black had planted on the lampshade to pick up what was on the screen.

"He's texting all right," Shields said, pointing at the image. "And look who he's messaging."

Black leaned in again, trying to make out the name. When he saw it, he leaned back and slapped the table.

"Jackpot," he said. "It's Roman."

CHAPTER 17

San Francisco, California

TATIANA TRUDGED UP THE STEPS on the Greyhound Bus, pausing to flash her ticket for the driver. She navigated to the back and sat down at a window seat. Clutching her bag to her chest, she studied the passengers as they boarded. After getting passed over by a handful of people, a girl who appeared to be in her early teens settled next to Tatiana.

The two girls remained silent until after the bus was loaded. As it chugged out of the station underneath a dusky sky, the girl cast a furtive glance at Tatiana. The driver addressed everyone over the intercom, giving the riders an idea of how much longer before they reached their next destination.

"We'll be stopping in Reno," he said. "If you need to use the restroom before then, I suggest you utilize the toilet in the back of the bus."

"I shouldn't have ordered this," the girl said aloud as she stared at her cup.

"Is it not good?" Tatiana asked.

"It's from a machine," the girl said, shaking her head. "In a world with a Starbucks on every corner, this stuff is barely above watered-down dirt. And now drinking it is going to mean I have to use that glorified porta-potty back there."

"I don't drink coffee," Tatiana declared.

The girl's eyes widened. "You don't drink coffee?"

"No."

"It's the only way I stay awake during the day. Well, that and the liquor—and the occasional extra pick-me-up."

"Pick-me-up?" Tatiana asked. "What's a pick-me-up?"

The girl eyed Tatiana closely. "Where are you from?"

"Here and there," Tatiana said, parroting her prescribed answer.

"I'm Amber," the girl said, offering her hand.

"Nice to meet you. I'm Emily," Tatiana said.

According to the general, Emily was the quintessential American name. "If you use your real name, they will be suspicious of you," he'd warned her. "But if you always use Emily, they won't think about it twice. America is a great melting pot, and they're so concerned with offending one another, even if they think you might not be one of them, they won't say anything."

Tatiana watched in amazement as Amber continued chatting away without even giving pause to the fact that her seatmate might not be an American. The general stressed that Americans were anything but accepting of foreigners.

"So do you understand what a pick-me-up is now?" Amber asked.

Lost in thought, Tatiana nodded absentmindedly. "Of course. That makes sense."

"Were you listening to me?" Amber asked.

Tatiana sighed and shook her head. "I'm sorry. I was thinking about something else. It's been a rough few weeks."

"You too, huh?"

Tatiana nodded. "If I told you what I was doing, you wouldn't believe me."

Amber shrugged. "I probably would. This world is a crazy place and full of people who want to hurt you."

Her sentiment is one the general repeated nearly every day. "The Americans want to bring harm to you and our citizens," he'd said. "It's a dangerous place with corrupt people running all branches of their government—and they must be stopped."

While Tatiana had heard this mantra repeated, she still had questions about it. "There are people who want to hurt you?"

Amber nodded. "That's why I'm running away."

"What kind of people?"

"Powerful people, rich people, poor people, men, women—it really doesn't matter. My parents didn't want me when I was a child, and so they threw me into the system. I've lived all over this country in some of the worst conditions imaginable. And when I told people in authority about what was happening, I was told to keep my mouth shut or else people would get hurt."

"The system?" Tatiana asked.

"Yeah, foster care. It's the worst."

Tatiana nodded as if she understood, but she didn't fully comprehend what *foster care* was. She'd never heard of such terms. And she certainly never knew parents getting rid of unwanted children was a common practice in the United States. In Russia, mothers and fathers used to sell their kids with alarming frequency to American couples eager to adopt, but a few years ago the president had put an end to it. There were still ways to sell a child into adoption, but it was risky, and people weren't interested in taking big chances, especially when the government was offering substantial sums of money for couples to have more children.

"What will you do now?" Tatiana asked.

"I'm not sure yet, but I'm sure not going to stick around and let anyone take advantage of me, if you know what I mean."

She had a good idea about what Amber was saying, so Tatiana nodded emphatically, hoping that the conversation didn't go any further. During her training, Tatiana had remained skeptical about everything the general had told her class regarding life in the U.S. If it was really that bad and Americans were as wealthy as they were portrayed, she wondered why they all didn't leave. But Amber didn't appear to have the means to travel abroad and stay there. Tatiana was quickly learning that life was far more complicated than when she was younger—and the world was far darker.

And I'm going to make it a better place, a place without some of these cruel people to torment kids like me. Papa will be proud of me.

CHAPTER 18

Washington, D.C.

BLACK PLACED HIS WATCH on his dresser and then eased beneath the sheets. He was exhausted from a long day, and a good night's sleep was at the top of his momentary wish list. Armed with knowledge that Gaither was working with Roman, Black could rest easy knowing that next steps for the Firestorm team would be straightforward when it came to dealing with the Missouri senator.

But there was still a nagging feeling that Black couldn't shake. He threw off the covers and sat upright. After snatching his phone off the bedstand, he dialed Shields's number.

"You do realize it's after 1:00 a.m., right?" she asked.

"Stop complaining," Black said. "I know you're up."

"You think that just because I know my way

around a mainframe computer that I'm some kind of night owl who guzzles lattes after midnight and never goes to bed before 3:00 a.m.?"

"That's exactly what I think you do."

"Well, you get no bonus points for having a grossly simplified characterization of me fed to you—and by me, no less."

"So, do you need a latte or an energy drink?" Black asked.

"I need you to leave me alone and get some sleep."

Black sighed. "I'm sorry. I knew I shouldn't have called. But I just can't help this nagging feeling that Gaither knows we're on to him."

"If he knew we were on to him, he wouldn't have called Roman."

"Only if he didn't think we were watching him," Black said. "He's paranoid and trying to alert Roman."

"But that doesn't mean Gaither knew we were watching him."

"No, it doesn't. But you know when you get that feeling when you're holding what you believe is a trump card but you think the other person might know?"

"I hate cards. They're so—"

"Predictable?"

"Most definitely. Give me a strategy game any day."

"Well, I feel like we might be coming across as

predictable," Black said. "And Gaither is going to do everything to bring chaos upon us. My promise to find the person responsible for shooting him might not be what he wants."

"Of course it isn't, if he's really guilty of orchestrating some illegal scheme to traffic young girls all over the world."

"So what do we do now?"

"The only thing we can do—wait."

Black got up and paced around the room. "I'm not sure which will kill me first: waiting for this to reach some resolution or one of Gaither's thugs."

"Just take it easy," Shields said. "Nobody knows where you live. Blunt saw to it that information is kept under wraps."

"I'm still sleeping with my Glock underneath my pillow."

Shields chuckled. "Would there ever be a reason not to?"

"Good point," Black said.

"Try to get some sleep. I'll update you in the morning with what this latte-drinking night owl learns before I go to bed at 3:00 a.m."

"Talk to you tomorrow," Black said before he hung up.

He climbed back into bed and checked his weapon.

Maybe I'm just paranoid.

Black struggled to go to sleep, his mind racing with all the possibilities of what Gaither might be up to. But after an hour, Black finally drifted off.

Yet it wasn't long before he sat bolt upright in bed, certain that he'd heard one of the floorboards creak.

Thinking quickly, Black stuffed a blanket and one of his pillows underneath the sheets, giving the illusion that he was in bed. He scrambled underneath the mattress and waited.

Ten minutes passed before he started to wonder if he was overreacting. Just as he was about to go investigate the noise, he saw the handle turn slowly and the door ease open. A man wearing dark clothes glided up to the foot of the bed. He pulled out his gun that had a silencer on it and fired two shots at where Black's head would've been.

"Huh," the man said as he strode up to the edge of the bed and ripped the covers back. That's when Black sprang into action.

Black shot the assassin in his leg. As he instinctively reached for the wound, Black fired three more shots, hitting the man twice more in his leg before finishing him off with a shot to the side of the head after he tumbled to the floor. Black wormed out from underneath the bed and stood over the man, blasting him again in the chest with a bullet just to make sure.

Once Black turned the light on, he kicked the gun away from the man and knelt to check his pulse. He was gone.

Black pulled out his phone and took a couple pictures of the man before sending them to Shields in a text.

She wrote back moments later. "This is not the kind of picture guys typically send to women this late at night."

"Most typical guys don't have an assassin invade their bedroom at night and try to kill them either."

He counted aloud. "Three, two, one . . ."

His phone rang with a call from Shields.

"Someone just tried to kill you?" she asked.

"That someone I just sent you a picture of," Black said. "I'm hoping you can run that image of him through your database and find out who he is."

"I can do that. Does he look familiar?"

"He's not the same guy who tried to kill me at Union Station, if that's what you mean," Black said. "This guy's eyes are quite memorable."

"I see that," she said. "Crystal blue."

"There aren't many people who know where I live, much less those who can get through my security system. He had to have some help."

"Good thing you trusted your gut."

"It's rarely wrong," Black said. "And now it's going to be hungry because I have to spend the rest of the night getting rid of this body."

"Need any help?"

Black chuckled. "You've got other fish to fry, like figuring out who this guy is. I'll take care of this on my own."

"Roger that. I'll be in touch."

After Black hung up, he wasted no time in enacting his protocol for body disposal. The process consisted of creating interference for all nearby closed circuit cameras before lugging the dead man down the steps in a large wagon topped with a cooler and several lawn chairs. He didn't figure he was likely to run into anyone in the elevators at 2:30 a.m., but there was always a chance.

And tonight was one of the nights he did.

The elevator stopped on the third floor and was boarded by a man with his shirt unbuttoned halfway and a pair of sunglasses sitting cock-eyed and clinging tenuously to his nose. With him was a pair of doting women.

Black scooted aside to make more room for them, hoping they wouldn't engage in conversation with him. But the man's breath smelled as if he'd spent most of his evening guzzling liquor as he staggered inside and leaned against the back wall.

He took his sunglasses off and used them to point at Black's wagon. "Kind of late for a picnic, isn't it?"

Black nodded and forced a smile, hoping the acknowledgment of the man's comment would end the prying.

"So, where you headed, pretty boy?" the drunk said. "Got anything in there for me?"

The man reached for the cooler and tried to open it. Black slammed his foot on the lid, refusing to even look at the man.

Incensed that he was denied a peek, he shrugged the two women off his arms and got in Black's face.

"Just who do you think you are?" the drunk said.

Black ignored the man again, looking straight ahead. Irked by the apparent disrespect, he stepped back before taking a swing at Black. He reacted quickly, putting his hand up to stop the attempted blow. Then he twisted the man's hand around, forcing him into submission and onto his knees.

Black leaned down and spoke in a low and measured tone. "I think I'm the man who could further embarrass you right now, but you're not really worth my time."

A ding signaled that the elevator had reached the lobby. As soon as the doors parted, the two girls hustled out and turned around to look at their escort.

"Have a nice night," Black said before turning the man's hand once more, resulting in a yelp of pain.

He scrambled to his feet and strode over to the girls, smoothing out his shirt and trying to act like nothing had happened.

Black hustled to his car and drove a half-hour south to Prince William Forest Park, where he dug a hole. Black knew it wasn't deep enough to bury the body without it ever being found, but he was exhausted and knew there was plenty of work to be done if he and the Firestorm team were going to successfully apprehend the people behind the trafficking ring.

Black returned to his apartment and reset his security system. After doing a thorough check of all the rooms, he crashed on the couch, passing out in a matter of minutes.

When he awoke, he wasn't certain if he was still dreaming. His blinds were closed, but there wasn't anything other than the glow of the city lights illuminating the edges around the window.

That's when he heard it again, the sound that startled him awake. Someone was pounding on his front door.

Black sat upright, yawned, and rubbed his eyes. He glanced at his watch.

Are you kidding me?

His clock read 4:30 a.m. He'd only been asleep for an hour.

Black lumbered toward the front door and groaned. He looked at the camera and noticed it was Shields.

"Do you know what time it is?" Black asked.

"I'm fully aware," she said. "Now, grab your go bag. We need to get moving."

Black squinted and shook his head. "Did I miss something?"

"Yeah," she said. "I'll fill you in once we get to my car."

"Seriously? Can you at least give me a clue as to what's going on?"

Shields sighed and set her jaw. "The feds are coming for you."

"For me? What on Earth for?"

"The attempted murder of Sen. Gaither and the murder of Capt. Watkins."

CHAPTER 19

BLUNT SPENT THE NEXT morning fielding calls from several high-ranking officials within various intelligence agencies to get his input on what might be the best way to capture Titus Black. While Blunt's leadership over the clandestine black ops group was one of the better kept secrets in Washington, he was still regarded as one of the best intelligence minds in the city. And given the circumstances, he wished he wasn't so highly regarded.

After finishing a call from someone at the FBI, Blunt sank into his chair at his office and turned on the television to see if there were any more reports breaking about Black's alleged crime. If Black wanted to disappear, he could. But Blunt needed one of his best assets pulling the curtain back on the apparent trafficking ring operating through the U.S. military. And Blunt hadn't heard from Black since the FBI fingered him as the assassin.

The news anchor blathered on about world markets

and stock trends for a few minutes before a bold graphic flashed up on the screen along with some dramatic music, signaling that a big piece of news was forthcoming.

"Law enforcement officials have released photos of the man they believe to be responsible for the attempted murder of Sen. Gaither yesterday as well as the death of Capt. Watkins at a welcome home rally for the Air Force pilot," the newscaster said in a somber tone.

A picture of Black flashed on the screen. Blunt breathed a sigh of relief when the image depicted was one of Black in disguise. In the photo, he had bleached-blond hair, a matching goatee, and contacts that turned his eyes brown.

Blunt chuckled at the attempt to assist the public in identifying the alleged culprit, who appeared to be an entirely different person.

That's real helpful.

"According to sources at the FBI, this man, Titus Black, is a former CIA operative who turned rogue several years ago and is a hitman for hire. Officials believe that Black may be connected to several other unsolved murders of political officials in Washington, including the death of longtime lobbyist Francis Norton, who was found dead under suspicious circumstances last month in his home overlooking the Potomac River."

Blunt shook his head and sighed. Someone was trying to cut Firestorm off at the knees—and there was no doubt who it was.

The anchor continued his report, which was a rehash of the shooting, preceded by a warning that viewer discretion was advised. Shaky footage taken by members of the audience showed the attack again, though any images of Titus Black were conspicuously missing.

"Officials found a sniper rifle with Black's fingerprints on it on top of the Museum of Natural Sciences and have released footage of him scoping out the area several hours before the event began," the newscaster said.

Before the report concluded, Blunt's phone buzzed. When he answered, Robert Besserman was on the other end.

"J.D., how are you getting along this morning?" he asked.

"I'd rather be on a sailboat in the Caribbean," Blunt said.

"Wouldn't you rather be doing that any day?"

Blunt grunted. "Here lately, I would. But there's important work to be done, and I can't entrust this work to anyone."

"Maybe not for long," Besserman said.

"What do you mean?"

"Gaither knows about Firestorm."

Slackjawed, Blunt shook his head. "How is that possible? There aren't more than a half dozen people who know about it and—"

"I don't know if someone told him or if he figured it out somehow. But he knows who's on the oversight committee for the black ops programs, and he's pressuring two of the members to bring it to an end. If Titus Black isn't captured and brought to justice, Gaither is threatening to expose everything."

"Oh, come on, Bobby. You know he didn't try to kill Gaither."

"Have you heard from Black?"

"Not yet. I'm sure he'll be impossible to find, even by me."

"Fine," Besserman said. "I'm doing my due diligence as requested by my fellow colleagues at other intelligence agencies. But if you don't want to tell me, I understand. I feel like Gaither has been playing a long game here, trying to set all the pieces in place before putting them into motion."

"Gaither knows we're on to him," Blunt said. "He's trying to eliminate everyone who could unmask him, which I don't think is all that many people."

"Based on what we have right now, we're going to have a very difficult time proving that he knew anything about that trafficking ring."

"I agree," Blunt said. "But we just need more

than what we have right now."

"What do we even have at this point? Some cell phone records? Grainy video footage? A few cryptic emails between him and Roman?"

"We're trying to set Gaither up, but we need a little bit more time."

Besserman sighed. "Unfortunately, that's not something I can afford to give you at the moment. When there's an attempt on the life of a U.S. senator, the FBI isn't going to sit on their hands just so we can trap someone, especially when he was the supposed intended target. They're going after the low-hanging fruit because they feel the pressure from the public, not to mention from the White House."

"I might be able to keep the president appeased if you can urge the FBI to relax since we know this isn't some conspiracy to kill Gaither."

"If I tell them that, they're going to want to know everything," Besserman said. "And I can't just hoard info. They expect us to share things, especially if it's going to lead to the apprehension and conviction of a killer."

"Stall them however you can," Blunt said. "I have an idea how I can steer them toward other leads. But you just have to do whatever you can to protect Firestorm. You know how important this team is to our national security interests."

"Indeed I do. I'll do the best I can, but I'm not

promising anything."

"We'll talk soon." Blunt hung up and then scrolled through his list of contacts in his phone before fingering Nate Miller's name. The reporter answered after the third ring.

"Senator Blunt, to what do I owe the pleasure of your call?" the reporter for *The Washington Post* asked.

"I'm honored that you picked up," Blunt said.

"Honored? Come on now, Mr. Blunt. Let's dispense with the false humility. I know you need something. What is it?"

"Look, I know someone tried to take you out, but I need a favor."

Miller huffed a soft laugh through his nose. "I just met with someone you might know a few days ago—and he told me if I wanted to live, I need to stop exposing corruption in the military."

"What about pulling back the covers on members of congress?"

"I don't think that'd be a good idea either at the moment."

"If you want to eliminate the threat altogether, I know how to achieve that."

"Sorry, Mr. Blunt. But I'm not interested," Miller said before he ended the call.

Blunt let out a string of expletives. He needed another plan—and fast.

CHAPTER 20

Washington, D.C.

BLACK DONNED A PAIR of aviator glasses and a stocking cap as he entered the store just after dark. He and Shields had spent most of the day holed up in a hotel room they paid for with cash. They had formulated a tentative plan but needed to connect with Blunt, waiting until nightfall to do so. Having long since ditched their phones to avoid being tracked by the FBI, they still needed to reach Blunt before taking the next steps. Black purchased a pay-as-you go phone and ducked out of the building, keeping a low profile and avoiding direct eye contact with any security cameras. He climbed into Shields's car and then dialed Blunt's secret burner cell, hoping the Firestorm director was available.

After the third ring, Blunt answered.

"Are you all right?" Blunt asked.

"In a manner of speaking," Black said.

"Physically, I'm fine except for some exhaustion after surviving an attempt on my life last night. Mentally, not so much. I've got a lunatic senator putting out hits on me while at the same time accusing me of trying to assassinate him. It's quite maddening at the moment."

"Gaither sent someone to kill you?"

"I had a bad feeling that something like that was going to happen," Black said before launching into a recap of the episode and the events that followed.

"I would say that I understand, but I don't," Blunt said. "I've only been hunted out in open waters by our government at the direct order of the president. But the two-pronged approach Gaither is employing to get you shows just how much thought he's put into making sure you don't expose him or, at the very least, aren't taken seriously."

Black let out an exasperated breath. "He's either thoughtful or he's desperate, throwing everything at me, including the kitchen sink. With that kind of tactic, he's just hoping something brings me down before he's exposed."

"Is Shields with you?"

"Yeah," Black said. "She was beating down my door in the middle of the night to get me out of there once she heard Gaither turned the tables on me and was spinning this story like I was the assassin."

"At least the media isn't using a current picture

of you," Blunt said. "Cable news might as well have posted a picture of Jo-Jo the Dog-Faced Boy in your place. The picture that's circulating makes you look like some younger version of Guy Fieri."

"I saw that picture and couldn't help but laugh. I have that going for me, I guess, but not much else."

"Well, there's more. I just spoke with Besserman, and he said he can help us if we get more proof of Gaither's involvement."

"That's a little difficult right now since the two agents you have who can do that are literally running for their lives from the same man accusing me of trying to kill him," Black said. "I swear if I took a shot at that criminal, I wouldn't have missed."

"I know this is frustrating, but you've gotta believe me when I say I'm doing everything I can. I even tried to get Nate Miller from *The Post* to help out, but he declined."

"He's probably just heeding my advice."

"Well, until we come up with something actionable, you and Shields need to get somewhere safe," Blunt said.

"That's why I called. I was hoping you might be able to give us directions to one of your safe houses."

"I'm not sure that's the best idea considering the way Gaither is unleashing all his fury on catching you and playing on public sympathy," Blunt said. "You need to get out of Washington—and far away from it."

"What do you suggest?"

"I can get you two out of the country."

"Out of the country?" Black said. "If anyone finds out we've left the U.S., we'll certainly look guilty."

"Not any guiltier than you look like right now," Blunt said. "Look, you two need to figure out a way to gather sufficient proof that Gaither knew what was going on with this trafficking ring. Once you do that, we can clear your name and put him away for good—in a place where he belongs. We'll talk soon."

Black hung up and pocketed his phone.

"Where to?" Shields asked as she put her rental car in gear and backed out of the parking spot.

"Leesburg Executive Airport," Black said. "Wheels up in an hour. Blunt will let us know where we're going once we get airborne."

"He's sending us somewhere without an extradition treaty, isn't he?" Shields asked.

Black shrugged. "He didn't say, but that would be my assumption. Right now, he's pretty worried that we're not going to have enough time to prove our innocence and gather the proof we need."

"I'll get to work on this as soon as we get in the air," Shields said, patting Black on the knee in a reassuring gesture. "We're going to figure this out."

"Of course we are," Black said.

But he didn't say it with any conviction. In an ironic twist, Black wondered if the only way out of the situation might be to actually kill Gaither. But regardless of how they planned to restore their name and put Gaither away, the degree of difficulty continued to climb with each passing minute.

CHAPTER 21

BLACK SCANNED THE AREA as Shields parked in a lot across the street from the Leesburg Executive Airport. They grabbed their gear and hustled toward the perimeter. While it was relatively quiet this time in the evening, Black didn't want to take any chances of being seen by airport personnel. He searched for a loose spot under the fence and slid beneath it before helping Shields get through.

They crouched low as they crept toward the hangar which housed Blunt's jet. A plane roared overhead as it lurched skyward and startled Shields.

"Don't be so jumpy," Black said, speaking in a hushed tone. "Nobody knows we're here, at least it doesn't appear that way. Once we get on the plane, we'll be fine."

"I'm not worried about the plane," she said. "The moment I step on that plane with a fugitive, I'm just as guilty. So, I'm more concerned about what will happen when we return—or if we'll even be able to return."

"Blunt's gonna figure out some way to get us back. You know we can find enough to put Gaither away. And if that doesn't work . . ."

"I know what you're implying by that last statement, but that kind of justice isn't going to get you your life back—or mine either. We need mountains of evidence to show Gaither is a conniving criminal as opposed to a sympathetic public servant."

"And we'll find it, but you can't waver now. If we do, he wins. And we can't let that happen. Where's Courageous Christina when we need her?"

Shields huffed a soft laugh. "I'm here. Just thinking I need more proof than courage at the moment."

"The hangar is about a hundred meters across the tarmac," Black said, pointing to it. "Do you think you can hustle with me over there so we can talk about your loss of nerve on the jet?"

"Fine," Shields said. "Let's do it."

"That's what I like to hear," he said. "On my mark. In three, two, one . . ."

Black stood and bolted across the runway toward a series of hangars. He glanced back to see Shields right behind him. When they reached the side of the building, they unlocked the door and entered. Blunt's pilot, Kyle Pratt, was going over his checklist for the Challenger 650. The three exchanged brief pleasantries before focusing on getting the plane ready. Pratt resumed his pre-flight checks, while Black and Shields weighed their gear and then loaded up.

"Don't you normally fly a Gulfstream?" Black asked as he walked up the steps.

Pratt looked up from his clipboard. "When we're on a sanctioned mission. This one doesn't fill that bill, so I'm using Blunt's private plane."

"I like it," Shields said.

"It also means I don't have a co-pilot," Pratt said.

"I don't care if you're blind as long as you can fly us outta here," Black said.

Pratt patted the side of the plane. "That shouldn't be a problem in this baby. Plus I know if something happens to me, I hear you know what you're doing in a cockpit."

"There might be some truth to that rumor."

Pratt grinned wryly. "And I'd prefer we not find out tonight if it's true."

"You and me both," Black said. "Now, where exactly are we going?"

"I filed a flight plan for Miami, but we're going much farther away than that," Pratt said. "Blunt told me he would text me the coordinates once we start taxiing. But we've got a full tank of gas and can get just about halfway around the world with only a couple stops."

Pratt worked over his gum as he returned to his duties.

Once everything was loaded, he alerted Black and Shields so they could get situated for the flight. The former fighter pilot eased the jet out of the hangar and onto the tarmac. However, an abrupt stop sent Black and Shields lurching forward and then whipping backward.

"What is it?" Black asked as he hustled up to the cockpit.

Pratt sighed and pointed at the baggage tug racing toward their plane. "It's Carl Berry, this airfield's own Barney Fife. He's a security guard who's a stickler for protocol. I'm sure he just wants me to fill out some paperwork or something. It'll only take me a minute to get rid of him."

Pratt cut the engine and opened the door. He descended the steps as Black and Shields looked on from inside the cabin.

"Good evening, Carl," Pratt said. "Is everything all right?"

Carl wrapped his hand around his gun, which was still holstered. He remained quiet, his eyes darting back and forth as if he was searching for something.

"Earth to Carl? Are you listening to me?" Pratt said, waving his hand in front of Carl's eyes.

"Yeah, I'm here," Carl said. "Who you got in there?"

"Now, Carl, how many times do I have to tell you that it's none of your business who I take and where I take them? Got that?"

Carl drew a long breath in through his nose and rubbed it with the back of his hand. He glanced over his shoulder before returning his gaze to Pratt.

"Don't be stubborn, Capt. Pratt," Carl said. "I know what you're up to."

"I'm just doing my job, Carl."

"And that's what I'm doing," he said before stealing another look down the runway. "Now, I need to inspect your cabin."

"Do you have a warrant?" Pratt asked.

Carl patted his sidearm. "I don't need one. Now if you'll excuse me, I need to take a peek at who's on board here."

"For goodness sake, can you just let us get on our way? We're on a tight timeframe."

"I'm sure you are," Carl said as he pushed his way past Pratt and walked up the steps.

As soon as Carl approached the plane, Black hustled back to his seat. When Carl appeared in the doorway, Black gave the security patrolman a friendly wave.

"Evening, sir," Black said with a deliberate nod. "What seems to be the holdup?"

"The holdup is *you*," Carl said, pointing his finger at Black. "You're not supposed to leave the country."

"Do you even know who this is?" Pratt asked. "This man is a decorated hero, and I'm supposed to take him to a secret location per my orders."

"Whose orders?"

"Does it matter?" Pratt asked. "It's all above your pay grade. Heck, it's way over mine, too."

Outside, the roar of engines speeding toward their position alarmed Pratt. He hustled down the steps and looked toward the far end of the airfield. Then he motioned for Black.

Carl grabbed Black's arm before he reached the bottom step. "Not so fast, my friend."

Black peered across the tarmac and saw a half dozen vehicles storming toward them. "That's not normal, is it, Carl?" Black asked.

"I think you know what this is about," Carl said as he nudged Black with his gun.

Black turned around and raised his hands. "Let's not do anything crazy."

A smile crept across Carl's lips as he basked in the moment of capturing Washington's most-wanted fugitive. However, that look dissolved when Shields addressed him from behind.

"If you want don't want eight pounds of carbon fiber shoved up your ass, I suggest you put your weapon down slowly and kick it aside," she said as she grabbed a fistful of his collar.

Carl knelt slowly and placed his gun on the ground. He slid the weapon aside with his foot, which Black pounced on.

"We also need the keys to your baggage tug there," Black said.

Shields slung their bags into the back as she slid onto the seat next to Black. "Do the right thing and tell them you never saw us. I can find out where you live."

Black watched the security guard swallow hard before wheeling the vehicle around and racing toward a gate at the back entrance. They both ducked as they crashed through it, shattering the padlock. Once they reached the road, Black grabbed a pair of chocks in the back and held them just above the gas pedal. He and Shields got out with their gear before he aimed the car down the straightaway. They hustled across the street toward Shields' rental car and watched as several FBI vehicles sped past them after the baggage tug, which was veering toward the woods.

Once they were out of sight, Shields pushed the ignition button and navigated back toward the main highway, which cut through the middle of Leesburg in an east-west direction.

"What to do now?" she said.

"Head back to Washington," Black said. "I've got an idea."

Shields sighed. "So much for getting out of town."

CHAPTER 22

BLACK GRABBED HIS solid-blue Washington Nationals cap out of his bag and tugged it down tight across his forehead. He suggested Shields tie her brunette hair up in a bun and wear her glasses. If they intended to stick around the capital, they needed to change their appearance at random intervals to keep throwing off the FBI agents scouring CCTV footage for them.

"What difference does this really make?" Shields asked. "We haven't switched vehicles yet, so once they spot us in this one, it'll be easy for them to track us."

"You said that you took your car to the dealership to get fixed, right?"

"Right, so what?"

"Is this a courtesy car? I mean, you didn't rent this did you?"

She shook her head.

"And you haven't paid for any repairs, have you?"

"Not yet," she said. "I don't normally pay until

it's completed."

Black slapped the dashboard. "Exactly, so they will be looking for us in your car, not this one. How will they have any idea that you had car trouble and are now driving a rental? No credit card records. No paper trail of any kind."

"So why do I have to put my hair up in a bun? I hate this look."

"Just go along with it and keep driving."

Black pulled out his phone and called *The Washington Post* switchboard. "I'm trying to reach Nate Miller," he said once the receptionist answered the phone.

Moments later, he listened to Miller's voicemail, which implored the caller to reach him on his cell phone for a more immediate response. Black took down the number and dialed it, but not before blocking his own so that it would appear as a private number on Miller's caller ID.

"Are you calling someone internationally?" Shields asked.

"I'm hiding my number from Miller," he said. "It'll make someone like him go crazy. He won't be able to resist the mystery of who's trying to reach him."

"I hope you're right."

After the eighth ring, Black's call went to

voicemail. He growled and redialed Miller.

"Unable to *resist the mystery*, huh?" she chided Black.

Black shot her a sideways glance. "Watch your speed," he said, ignoring her dig. "We don't want your lead foot to be the reason we get captured."

"This foot is made out of carbon fiber, thank you very much. And as it stands right now, it's the reason we escaped."

Black chuckled. "That guard would've wilted if you told him that you had magic pixie dust that would grow a goiter on his nose if he didn't do what you said."

"The world will never know now, will it?"

Black redialed Miller's number, which went straight to voicemail this time.

"I'm hoping this plan materializes soon so I'm not driving around town all night," Shields said.

"Just be patient," Black said as he made another attempt to reach Miller.

She cocked her head and flashed him a wry smile. "Third time's the charm, right?"

This time, Miller picked up, his voice blaring over the speaker. "Who is this? And why do you keep calling me?"

"This is your friend from the coffee shop the other day," Black said.

"At least I know your name now."

"The whole world does."

"The whole world also thinks you're an assassin," Miller said.

"Why don't you prove them wrong," Black suggested.

"How exactly am I supposed to do that?"

"We need to meet ASAP. I have something to give you."

"I can't meet right now," Miller said. "I'm at the Nats game. They're playing the Braves, and my team is winning."

"The Nats are beating the Braves?"

Miller chuckled. "Not a chance. I'm from Atlanta, mystery man. I thought you would've known that about me."

"I didn't dig that deep. What inning is it?"

"The fourth, and the Braves are winning 7-1."

"Don't go anywhere. I'll contact you when I get there with further instructions."

"Who says I want to help you?"

"You're a good journalist, Nate. I'm sure you want the truth to come out about what Gaither and his minions are doing overseas and why he had a staged assassination attempt."

"The funny thing is *that* is the kind of journalist that I am. But someone I know told me to back off of this story if I wanted to live. I've moved on."

"Things have changed."

"For you, maybe. But not for me. I'm afraid that you'll have to find yourself another reporter to do your bidding."

Miller ended the call. Black let out a long breath and stared out the window.

"That was your great plan?" Shields asked. "Get Nate Miller to write an exposé that exonerated us?"

"You got a better one at this point?"

She nodded and grinned.

"So where are we going?"

"We're going to Nationals Park," she said.

CHAPTER 23

SHIELDS TWEAKED THE VOLUME in her coms and sent out a test message. Black's voice boomed, echoing in her ear piece. She pulled down on the bill of her cap, her eyes darkened by the shadow cast on them. After locating Miller, she settled into a few rows behind him. Most fans had conveniently cleared out as the Braves held a 10-2 lead, making it easy for her to view Miller.

When the next vendor strolled by hawking his beer, she ordered two and asked him to send one to Miller. The man eyed her closely and didn't agree until she gave him a five-dollar tip.

He hustled over to Miller and handed him the enormous thirty-two ounce beer. Miller turned around in his seat, and the vendor pointed at Shields. She forced a smile and gave him a friendly wave.

"All right, Operation Bud Light has commenced," Shields said. "It won't take long now."

* * *

BLACK PULLED UP THE ZIPPER on his janitorial coveralls and then used the mop handle to wheel the bucket of murky water along the concourse.

"Find the nearest bathroom to Section 113 on the mezzanine level," she said.

"Copy that," Black said as he plodded toward the area.

He positioned his bucket just inside the men's restroom door and started to clean up around the sinks.

Another janitor appeared in the doorway a couple minutes later with his own bucket. "Did Arnold assign you to this bathroom?"

Black shook his head. "No, it was the head guy."

"Mr. Darlington?"

"Yeah, that's the one," Black said.

The man shrugged, spun, and headed out the door.

After fifteen minutes, he heard Shields come in clear over his ear piece. "He's on the move. I repeat: the target is on the move."

Black strode over to the entrance and waited for Miller. Once he walked inside, Black slapped a "cleaning in progress" sign on the door and locked it with the deadbolt. After everyone had cleared out except for Miller, Black leaned against the sink, waiting for Miller to turn around from the stalls. When the reporter spun on his heel and headed for the exit, Black caught him.

"You know it's not polite to leave the restroom without washing your hands, though I hear that's a common habit among Braves fans," Black said.

Miller froze. He cast a quick glance over at Black before sprinting toward the exit. Black beat the reporter to the spot and crossed his arms, creating an imposing presence.

"I told you that we needed to talk," Black said.

"Look, I appreciate your tenacity, but I want to get back out there and finish watching the game."

"And I'll let you—after we're done with this brief but very important conversation."

Miller sighed and stared at the upper corner of the room. "I already told you I'm not interested in helping you. You were the one who helped me see what I was getting myself into."

"That's before I knew what I know now."

"Yeah, and what you know now is that someone is framing you for the assassination of Capt. Watkins and if I don't help you, there's a strong possibility you'll end up dead."

"That's it in a nutshell."

Miller shook his head. "I'm not going to foist some hoax on the American people just so you can skate for this. Not gonna happen."

"Just take a look at this and tell me what you think?" Black said, offering Miller a thumb drive. "It's going to blow your mind. And it's got all the elements of Pulitzer prize-winning stories every reporter dreams of: innocent people being harmed, a threat that needs to be neutralized, and corrupt politicians spearheading the entire thing."

Miller pushed Black's hand aside, refusing to take the device. "Sorry, not interested. Now, can I please get back to watching the game?"

"Not until you take this," Black said, keeping his right hand outstretched with the drive resting on his palm. "What's it gonna hurt to take a look?"

Miller snatched it from Black's hand before pocketing the memory stick. "Fine. Now will you move, please?"

"I hope you're serious about looking into this. You don't want to miss this story. If you're not the one to tell it when it breaks, you're going to regret it."

* * *

NATE MILLER FISHED his cell phone out of his pocket and punched in 911. He took a deep breath before hitting the send button.

"Nine one one, what's your emergency?" the dispatcher asked.

"I'm at Nationals Park, and I just saw Titus

Black, the wanted fugitive."

"Are you certain, sir?"

"Yes, he's here, and he's dressed in a janitor's coveralls and is currently on the mezzanine level."

"Copy that, sir. I'll let the authorities know immediately. Please stay on the line."

The line went silent as Miller paced around the concourse. He slipped his phone back into his pocket and backed into a little nook that gave him a little bit of cover from the men's restroom entrance. About thirty seconds later, Black walked out and checked over his shoulder before heading toward the exit. He was pushing his bucket with his head down, virtually invisible to all the fans streaming toward the exit as the game approached the ninth inning with the Nats trailing by eight runs.

However, he spun on his heels in a quick u-turn when he noticed several armed security guards walking toward him and scanning the crowd.

Miller smiled and pulled out his phone, eager to record the capture of the elusive Titus Black. Despite the sure-fire award-winning story that fell into Miller's lap, he still had a hard time believing that this was the same man who captured Capt. Watkins just a week ago and then shot him just over twenty-four hours ago. It seemed unlikely that he would travel halfway across the world to rescue the man only to kill him on stage with Senator Gaither in a botched assassination attempt, but little surprised Miller these days. He surmised that Black had warned him to stay out of it because he didn't want anyone else poking around on the story. And Miller figured if he was wrong, he could always write the follow-up exposé revealing how dark and twisted the military and intelligence community was.

A perfect two-for-one.

Miller struggled to keep up with Black's torrid pace. He had long since ditched his bucket and was pulling away from the officers. Sirens wailed in the distance, signaling just how serious this situation was.

Miller followed the officers until he noticed a trio of Metro police officers racing toward Black. He paused for a moment and surveyed the two groups pursuing him. Then Black darted up the steps toward the third level.

Miller did his best to keep Black in view, but the agent flung himself over the railing and disappeared into the darkness.

Where'd he go?

Dashing up the steps, Miller kept recording and hoped he caught something on tape. When he reached the top step, he panned the area below. With mouths agape, the cops all stared at the dim concourse below, which was devoid of anyone sprinting away by himself.

"Where the hell did he go?" one of the officers asked.

The other men shrugged and let out a string of expletives before one of the men snatched the walkie-talkie off his belt.

"We lost him," the officer said. "He flipped off the railing on the top level, and he's gone. Maybe one of the patrols on the outskirts of the stadium can spot him."

The officer described Black's clothing, but Miller was sure that the fleeing operative had stripped off the coveralls and was wearing something else by now.

Miller turned off his recording and walked down the steps, realizing there wasn't going to be a dramatic moment to capture on video. At least, he wasn't going to see it if there was.

He shoved his phone into his pocket and felt the thumb drive Black had given him.

I guess it wouldn't hurt to at least take a look at this.

Miller went home, elated over the Braves' trouncing of the Nationals, yet disappointed that he'd betrayed Black. But there was a way to make it up to him: Look at the contents of the thumb drive.

Miller inserted the device into his computer and started to sift through the files. It didn't take long before his eyes widened and his mouth dropped.

Are you kidding me?

Miller called his editor to tell him a synopsis of what was contained on the drive.

"I'll have a story for you tomorrow," Miller said before hanging up.

He was right. This is Pulitzer prize-winning material.

CHAPTER 24

Washington, D.C.

TATIANA SMILED AS SHE twirled across the stage to the captivating sounds of Pyotr Tchiakovsky's Swan Lake ballet. She hadn't felt this carefree and happy since that day in Bali at the beach when she was going to eat ice cream with her new friends. That seemed like a lifetime ago.

But as she leaped into the air and thrust her arms out, everything seemed to fade away like a distant memory. Even the girl she stabbed to death the night before so she could dance in this special performance. As Tatiana went to bed the night before, all she could see was the tortured dancer's face as she bled to death, begging Tatiana to stop while gasping for one last breath. Now, it was like a clean slate. One more person to kill and Tatiana could go home to be with her family. However, there was still work to be done, a dance to be mastered, a weapon to plant.

After one of the breaks, the instructor called Tatiana over.

"Emily, I seem to be missing your parental consent form," the woman said. "Would you mind taking this home to your parents and having them sign it before tomorrow night's performance?"

"Of course," Tatiana said.

"Thank you," the woman said. "I'd hate for you to miss it because of this. The passion that's expressed as you float across the floor is contagious."

Tatiana nodded. "That's so kind of you, ma'am. I appreciate that."

"I hope that inspires you to continue dancing. I know a lot of girls quit at this age because they're not going to make it. But I think that's silly if you really love something. And I can tell you love to dance."

"I love to perform," Tatiana said with a wink. "The applause makes all the hard work—the long nights at rehearsal and the calluses on my toes—worth it."

"As long as you find joy in it, I guess that's as good of a reason as any to dance."

"Don't get me wrong," Tatiana said. "I love dancing. But an audience makes it that much more enjoyable."

"Well, it's quite obvious that you've been trained by some very competent teachers. Your technical skill is excellent. And your posture? I wish I could get half the girls in my classes to carry themselves like that. If you don't mind me asking, where did you train?"

"Here and there," Tatiana said. "We've moved around a lot."

"I see. Well, don't forget to bring that form back. Whoever designated you as an alternate made a huge mistake. I'm glad to see that was rectified since Hannah didn't show up today. We needed an extra dancer, and if you hadn't been here, I would've had to have adjusted a large portion of the choreography."

Tatiana flashed a smile. "I'm glad to help. See you tomorrow—with a signed form."

"Ready for one more run through?" her teacher asked.

Tatiana nodded. "Of course."

"All right, everybody," the teacher said. "Let's take it from the top. Places!"

A wide grin spread across Tatiana's face. She took a deep breath as she assumed her opening position. Once all the girls were in place, the orchestra began playing, setting the dance into motion.

As she whirled past her teacher, Tatiana winked.

Enjoy it while you can because this will be the last time you see me dance this way.

Only one more day before Tatiana could go home. And she couldn't wait.

CHAPTER 25

CHRISTINA SHIELDS STILL HADN'T grown accustomed to the stares she received while out in public, her prosthetic right leg broadcasting her mishap as if it were a breaking news segment on television. Even when she wore pants and the combination of carbon fiber and titanium weren't visible, she still sensed people eyeing her closely. But for all her insecurity about the appearance of her lower extremities, none of that changed the fact that she still possessed blazing speed.

When she noticed Black in trouble at the stadium, she knew she needed to sprint out of there before Nate Miller put two and two together. The attractive woman, the extra large beer, the trip to the bathroom—if he realized that she was working with Black, Miller would report her to the authorities as well as some kind of accomplice. And if she was going to be able to help Black now, it wouldn't be by serving as his chauffeur. She figured she'd be better served misdirecting all the entities hunting for him, at least until she was able to dig up the proof necessary to implicate Senator Gaither.

She tried their coms, a shot in the dark considering she had no idea where he was or if he'd been captured.

"Black, do you read me?" she called.

Nothing.

"Come on, Black. Tell me you're okay."

Still nothing.

She opened the police scanner app on her phone and listened as Metro police spoke in coded language. Growing up as the daughter of a sheriff in small town Georgia, Shields spent plenty of nights with her father at the station. Despite her mother's objections, Shields scheduled at least one ride-along with her father every week, serving the two-fold purpose of satiating her desire to be around law enforcement and getting some one-on-one time with her dad.

"We've got a 10-29F near Nationals Park," the dispatch said, crackling over the speaker. "It isn't known if the subject is armed, but he's considered dangerous. If you spot him, do not approach, and wait for backup. I repeat, do *not* approach."

At least Black's still on the lam.

Shields wheeled her car around, escaping the rather sparse crowd leaving the stadium parking lot in a matter of minutes. Just before entering the stadium, she and Black had discussed the protocol in the event that they got separated. And she was headed straight to the rendezvous point. However, as she turned onto one of the surface streets by the stadium, traffic ground to a halt.

She rolled down her window, craning her neck to see what was causing the hold up. Then she noticed a police officer lumbering along the line of cars, illuminating the front and back seats of each automobile.

"Is everything all right, officer?" she asked, feigning concern and curiosity.

"Been a lot of drunks lately getting in accidents leaving the stadium," he said as he stopped by her car. "Just trying to make sure we're keeping the city's roads safe."

"I understand."

The officer started to walk away and then froze. "You wouldn't mind popping your trunk, would you?"

"Of course not," she said as she reached for the latch.

Seconds later, the trunk flew open. He poked his head inside and then slammed the door shut. Slapping the side of her car twice, he continued down the long line toward the next automobile.

"You're good to go, lady," the officer said.

Shields let out a sigh of relief.

That guy would've never made it at as a Lowndes County Sheriff's Deputy.

The nonchalant nature of the stop coupled with the fact that they were still performing such a check signaled to Shields that Black had evaded capture. But where he was remained a mystery.

She wanted to call him but opted to text instead in case the noise from the cell phone ring gave him away.

Using her thumbs, she pounded out the address for Brook Hill Park in Georgetown and sent it to him. He wrote back and said he'd be there in half an hour.

Shields needed ten minutes to reach a nearby Chinese restaurant about two blocks from the park where Black was supposed to be. If she had her druthers, she would've picked him up. But traveling together made them easier to find since a full manhunt had commenced.

She dug into her purse and collected two hundred dollars for Black, along with a fake ID she found in his go bag.

After studying the menu for a few minutes, she placed an order for herself and then added a to-go order for another address. When the delivery guy prepared to leave, she grabbed him by his jacket.

"Are you the one delivering that food to the

park?" she asked.

The guy scowled as he glanced down at the piece of paper with the address scrawled on it. "Yeah, I guess I am. What's it to you?"

"Take it to the bench on the west side, and I also need you to add something else to this delivery," she said with a wink as she handed him a small box.

He withdrew, throwing his hands in the air in a gesture of surrender. "Now, look, lady. I don't mean to be rude, but I don't make extra deliveries for customers."

With a folded twenty dollar bill tucked between her index and middle fingers, she waved it at him.

"It's not illegal," she said. "It's just a special thank you gift for my friend."

"Your friend? The homeless guy sleeping on the bench?"

"I know what it looks like but—"

He defiantly shook his head. "Sorry, ma'am. Not gonna do it. It ain't that far. Deliver your own special thank you gift in person."

"I can't do that."

The delivery man crinkled up his nose and glared at her. "Why not? Is your leg broke?"

"As a matter of fact, it is." Shields sighed, hiking up her pants leg.

"I'm sorry, ma'am. I—"

"Don't worry about it," she said before placing the money back in her purse. "I didn't want to have to do this, but I guess desperate times call for desperate measures. Would you do it for a hundred?"

The delivery guy leaned forward, attempting to peer into her purse. She snapped it shut and glared at him.

"Did your mama ever teach you any manners? Never snoop into a woman's purse."

He snatched the one hundred dollar bill out of her hand. "Okay, I'll do it."

He grabbed the box and started to peek inside.

Shields slapped his hand. "No peeking. That's the deal. Besides, you're better off not knowing what's in there."

He rolled his eyes and let out an exasperated breath before collecting everything and spinning toward the door. Shields waited until he was gone before she strode after him. She stopped and shot a glance over her shoulder, noticing the restaurant owner holding the phone close to his ear and speaking in hushed tones. That was a stark departure from his boisterous personality he held when she first walked into the store.

Shields put her head down and walked swiftly toward her car. The pedestrian traffic along the sidewalk was nominal just after 10:30 p.m. on a Friday, but it was the weekend. She passed a Metro police foot patrolman strolling nonchalantly past her in the opposite direction. She cut her gaze toward him before bouncing it back to the ground in front of her.

Shields looked over her shoulder at the storefront window to her right, stealing a peek at the officer's reflection. He stopped abruptly and yanked his walkie-talkie off his belt as dispatch was squawking. Shields couldn't make out everything, but she thought she heard dispatch say "10-66", police code for "suspicious person."

When he finished listening to the message, he lowered it from his ear and started scanning the area. Shields picked up her pace and didn't look back for several seconds. Then she looked behind her when she heard a woman scream.

"Hey, watch it," she said. "You almost made me spill my coffee."

The officer had broken into a dead sprint and was barreling straight toward Shields.

CHAPTER 26

BLACK HUNG BACK in the shadows while waiting for the delivery guy to arrive. His coms hardly had any battery life left in them, and he needed to conserve that as much as possible in the event of a true emergency. For the time being, he could communicate with Shields via texting. And as much as he needed her to help him navigate the onslaught of law enforcement beating every bush and turning over every rock to find him, Black knew she was most valuable at the moment behind her keyboard and gathering damning evidence on Gaither.

I can hold these guys off long enough for Shields to work her magic.

After a few minutes, a sloppily dressed man in his early twenties parked his car along the curb and put on his flashers. He climbed out toting a plastic bag. Black made eye contact with the guy and nodded.

"Are you—" the delivery man asked, fishing out the receipt from the bag, "Dale Murphy?"

"Guilty as charged," Black said, trying to keep a straight face. By the serious manner in which the guy asked the question, it was apparent that he had no idea who Dale Murphy was. Black had listened to Shields talk incessantly about her dad's favorite baseball player, someone she'd never even seen play in person. According to her, Murphy belonged in the hall of fame and was the greatest Atlanta Braves player in the history of the franchise. And she just wouldn't shut up about it whenever the topic came up.

Black smiled as he took the food.

"She also wanted me to give you this," the man said, handing a small box to Black.

Black nodded and thanked the man, who didn't move. "If you're wanting a tip, you're gonna be standing there a while."

The man growled as he spun on his heels and hustled back over to his car. After he was out of sight, Black returned to the shadows and opened his gift from Shields.

Perfect.

Inside the box, he found a gun, a fake ID with one of his many aliases, and a thousand dollars in hundred dollar bills rolled up tightly. He needed to find some place to lay low for the night. There were a few low-rent hotels by Washington's standards a couple blocks north of his location.

Black ate a couple bites of his food before giving it all to a homeless man begging just outside the park on the street corner. Then Black headed for the hotel. He strolled along the sidewalk, acting casually and trying not to be suspicious. However, he recognized he needed to change tactics when he looked in the side mirror of a nearby parked car and noticed a dark SUV creeping behind him.

Black pulled his phone out, pretending as if he was answering a call. He threw his head back and feigned a laugh. But when he glanced in another mirror, he saw the agents in the vehicle easing up behind him weren't taking the bait.

He kept walking before darting toward the park. Hurdling the wrought iron fence, he sprinted across the grass, using the shadows cast by the trees as cover. When he reached the center, he dashed to his right and back out onto the sidewalk. With no immediate signs of any agents around him, Black found an alleyway and ducked into it.

Weaving through a maze of restaurant dumpsters and cars jammed into every available space behind the buildings, Black didn't stop until he found a good hiding spot behind a transformer and a stack of crates. He pulled out his phone and called Shields.

Come on, come on. Pick up.

The call went to voicemail. He put in his coms

and spoke in a soft tone.

"Shields, do you copy?"

Silence.

"Shields, do you copy?"

Still no response.

He waited a minute before he turned off his coms and tucked them back into his pocket.

Black scanned the area, looking for an open door that would give him access to one of the nearby buildings. Everything appeared secured shut, and there weren't any smoking restaurant workers in the alley at the moment. It was eerily quiet.

Black eyed a nearby fire escape and considered climbing it, but about the time he was ready to make a move, a pair of FBI agents entered the area. While he considered making a run for it, Black knew they would shoot first. If he was being regarded as that dangerous of a person, no law enforcement officer would think twice about shooting him.

And even though Black was armed, he wasn't about to kill someone who was just doing their job.

He listened as the two agents discussed their strategy.

"What are you thinking?" one of the men asked.

"He probably doubled back somewhere and is long gone," the other man answered.

"There's just nowhere to go here."

"Unless he went up."

"Briggs is checking the roofs around here in case our guy chose that option."

"I want to do our due diligence and check this alley."

"Want me to come with you?"

Squawking on their coms made them both stop. Black couldn't tell what was going on as both men put a finger to their ears.

"Go, go, go," one agent said. "I'll make a quick sweep and meet you back at the car."

After one of the agents left, the other man crept along the alley, his gun trained toward the ground. Black watched as the agent followed procedural methods to clear the area. As he eased behind a stack of pallets, he disappeared from Black's line of sight. Black started to get concerned after a few seconds when the man hadn't reappeared.

Where did you go?

Black felt the muzzle of a gun press against his head.

"Don't move a muscle," the man said.

CHAPTER 27

SHIELDS RACED ALONG the sidewalk, searching for a way to turn the tables on the officer chasing her. She knew she could outrun him, but eventually he'd have help. Up ahead, she spotted a construction dumpster situated along the edge of the road. She always hated happening upon those monstrous steel trash cans while navigating surface streets, but now she was happy to see one.

Darting behind it, she crouched low and waited for the officer to round the corner in pursuit. She listened intently and heard his approaching footfalls. Gearing up for the confrontation, she grabbed hold of the handle to brace herself. The moment he appeared, she thrust her leg out in front, tripping him up and sending him sprawling across the pavement.

Shields snatched his walkie talkie off his belt and sprinted away. As she ran, she placed the speaker to her ear, listening for what they were saying about Black. She quickly gathered that there were several FBI agents in the area chasing after him.

"Suspect spotted on the northwest corner of Wisconsin and R streets," she said into the walkie talkie. "And we've got an 11-87 on the northeast corner of Wisconsin and S."

That ought to confuse them for a while.

While working with her dad, she kept a running list of all the police codes she'd heard while hanging out with him. The only one that never came across the airwaves? The 11-87, which was used whenever a bomb was found.

The diversion worked to perfection, drawing both Metro police and FBI agents into the same general vicinity. Wherever Black was, he should've been able to get away with relative ease now.

She hustled to her car, putting her coms into her ear as she did.

"Black, can you hear me?" she asked.

Nothing.

"If you're able to, give me some kind of signal that you're out there and okay."

More silence.

She waited for another half-minute before pocketing the device and pulling out her cell phone. As she merged into traffic, she took a hard right and decided to make a drive around the perimeter of the area just in case she could be of any assistance. She dialed his number and begged for him to pick up. The line rang and rang, but he didn't answer.

She let out a string of expletives before tossing the phone aside in disgust.

Where are you, Black?

CHAPTER 28

BLACK DIDN'T EVEN TWITCH as the gun barrel dug into his skull. One false move and his life would be over, enough motivation for him to resist the urge to even raise his hands. The man grabbed a fistful of Black's collar and jerked him to his feet.

The agent shoved Black toward the wall. "Keep your hands where I can see them, and turn around slowly."

Black complied, raising his hands as he turned around. When he locked eyes with the agent, Black's mouth fell agape.

"Huxley?" Black asked, his eyes bulging out.

The FBI agent glanced back down the alley before fixing his gaze on Black. "I know it's been a while since we've seen each other, but I didn't expect it to be like this."

"You know this is all utter bullshit, right?" Black asked, keeping his hands raised.

Nick Huxley gestured for Black to put them

down. "When I heard we were coming over here as part of a manhunt, I knew I had to find you first. The things they're saying about you—"

"They're all lies," Black said. "Besides, if I wanted to nail that bastard Gaither, I wouldn't have hit him in the arm."

"I know. None of this has been adding up for me, even as the story within the bureau is that you're some rogue agent. I can't believe how many of our guys are swallowing this whopper of a tale whole."

"Look, I want to tell you the entire story, but I'll never get to if you don't help me get out of here."

"Who's responsible for all this?"

"That's what I'm trying to find out. This has nothing to do with some plot to kill Gaither, but everything to do with him. He's either directing or a part of a trafficking ring of some sort, which is utilizing our military's airplanes to transport young girls all over the world. I'd love to tell you more, but I've really got to get moving."

"Who else knows about this?"

"Not many people yet, but we intend on letting as many people as possible know once we've got some irrefutable evidence. Now, will you help me?"

"Of course," Huxley said. "I hope you don't mind tight spaces because the only way we're getting you out of here is in the trunk of my car."

"You remember I'm claustrophobic, right?"

"How could I forget?" Huxley said. "It was fun locking you in the closet that day."

"Still not funny—and I'm still mad about it."

Huxley smiled. "Well, maybe you'll forgive me once you share some space with my tire iron and spare."

"As long as it gets me out of here alive, I'll do it."

"Excellent. Now stay close, but stay down in case I run into any other fellow agents."

By the time they reached Wisconsin Street, the two blocks north of them were teeming with law enforcement officials from every agency in the city.

Huxley glanced at Black. "My car is right there. Just walk casually with me to the back of it."

As they strode toward Huxley's black sedan, he activated the trunk, popping it up. When they reached the automobile, they both looked around to make sure no one was watching them before Black climbed in.

"There's a blanket back there in case you get cold," Huxley said.

Black sighed. "My body temp is the least of my worries right now. Just keep me alive, all right?"

"I'll do my best," Huxley said.

Black tried to get as comfortable as possible as Huxley seemed to hit every pot hole possible as he left the area. After a few minutes, the car came to a halt and seemed to idle for an abnormally long time. As

Black started to wonder what was happening, he heard a man's voice just outside the car.

"Evening, officer," Huxley said. "What's this traffic stop all about?"

"Just a routine Friday night check," the man said. "Trying to make sure everybody gets home safe."

"Looks like we have the same goal then," Huxley said. "Nick Huxley, FBI."

After a brief moment, Huxley groaned. "Do you have to shine that thing in my eyes? I'm actually heading home after my shift ended."

"Sorry, our orders are to search every vehicle."

"Without probable cause?" Huxley asked. "You might want to be careful about how you proceed tonight. I'm fine with it, of course, but you could miss out on a conviction without following proper procedure."

"Agent Huxley, can I ask you a question?"

"Shoot."

"Do I ever come to your place of work and tell you how to do your job?"

"No, but I just—"

"Then let me do mine. Now, if you don't mind, I need you to go ahead and pop the trunk for me."

Black swallowed hard. He had to act fast.

The trunk creaked as it opened. Black had yanked on the seat back, granting him access to the back row. He squirmed through the slot and eased onto the floorboard.

"See," Huxley said. "Nothing to worry about. Now will you let me go on my way?"

The officer tossed Huxley's jumper cables and jack around before latching the trunk shut. "Sorry to trouble you, agent. But I'm sure you understand. Just following protocol and all."

Huxley put the car into drive. Black lurched backward, banging his head against the seat. After a couple minutes, Black peered up from the back.

"Is it safe yet?" he asked.

"It's safe," Huxley said. "But stay there just in case I'm caught on camera."

"Roger that," Black said.

"So, where am I taking you?"

"We've got a safe house in the city that nobody knows about. It's a place we can go to when everywhere else is compromised."

"What's the address?"

"How about I just tell you how to get there so you don't have a digital record of visiting our place?" Black suggested.

"Good idea. And this is why you made it as an agent with the agency and I never did."

"The bureau isn't anything to scoff at," Black said, trying to downplay his friend's compliment.

"That's not what you said when my application

was rejected," Huxley said.

"That was a long time, Nick. When are you ever gonna let that go?"

"When you apologize."

"I've told you I'm sorry at least a hundred times. Quite frankly, I'd call you up to grab a beer more often if you didn't always find some way to dredge this up."

"Keep your shirt on," Huxley said. "I'm just bustin' your chops."

Black proceeded to give Huxley the address for the safe house. Ten minutes later, Black bid his friend farewell after thanking him profusely.

With his head down, Black hustled up the steps to the apartment and entered a code on the access pad, unlocking the door. He slipped inside and strode across the room in search of the light switch when he heard a click and froze.

The lights came on, and there was Shields training her weapon on him.

She let out a sigh of relief and tucked her gun into her shoulder holster. "I wish you would've called."

"I tried, but you didn't pick up."

She picked up her phone. "Must've had a poor signal. But I'm glad you're here."

"Figure anything out yet?"

"As a matter of fact, I did. And you're not gonna believe what I found."

CHAPTER 29

THE NEXT MORNING, BLUNT awoke to the sound of his phone vibrating on the table next to his bed. He groaned as he leaned over to answer the call. It was 5:30 a.m. And while he had planned on connecting with Besserman first thing this morning, Blunt wanted to call around 7:00 a.m. at the earliest.

"You do realize it's still very much dark outside and I haven't consumed an ounce of coffee yet," Blunt said as he answered.

"Believe me when I say this that I wouldn't be calling you this early if I didn't have to," Besserman said. "I need my beauty sleep too."

"Well, I guess we should get down to business since neither one of us is getting any sleep this morning."

Besserman sighed. "Look, I don't know any real easy way to say this, but I've got every agency with more than two letters slapped together leaning on me to get some meaningful intel about your agents' whereabouts. Firestorm is still secretive, but every director wants me to use my intelligence resources to help them out. Now, I know you might feel like you're betraying them, but—"

"I'm gonna save you a lot of time right there, Bobby. I have no idea where they are."

"Not even a hunch?"

"I received a text from them last night telling me to check my email because they had sent me some files."

"Is this something I can use to stall all these agencies?"

Blunt drew a deep breath and exhaled slowly. "I hope so. But I'm going to need you to get this to one of your best analysts who can break it down."

"What's the problem?" Besserman asked.

"Shields was able to decrypt some of the files, but there are plenty of others that she can't crack. She said it was something to do with needing more computing power. I don't know. Just some mumbo jumbo jargon that I don't understand. But I'm hoping you'll be able to rectify this problem."

"I've got an ace analyst who I can send the file to once you forward it along to me. I might be able to use the possession of this alleged evidence to buy you some more time, but it's not going to be easy. The president wants a win, and he wants it right away."

"What kind of *win* is he looking for?" Blunt asked. "The kind that makes him look good? Or the kind that exposes corruption in the U.S. military?"

"I think you know the answer to that one."

"Well, I'm not about to let one of my men take the fall for a crooked politician fattening his wallet while innocent children are taken advantage of in the most egregious of ways."

"Look, I know you and Gaither have a past when you were serving in the senate, but don't let that cloud your judgment. He's not always—"

"That's not what this is about," Blunt said. "This is about justice. Justice for all the kids who have been ripped from their homes and flown to destinations all over the world. It's an unconscionable act that you and I shouldn't stand for, no matter what Washington powerbroker is pulling the strings."

"I wholeheartedly agree with you."

Blunt cocked his head to one side. "Why do I get the feeling that there's a *but* coming?"

"Because it is. But the truth is we can't just take down Gaither on what we've got. And they've got a mountain of evidence against you. And it's all circumstantial. However, if this thing were to get to trial, I'm not sure I would like your chances. Have you seen how upset the whole world seems to be over an attempted murder by a secret black ops agent?"

Blunt waved his hand dismissively as he paced around his office with his phone plastered to his ear. "Bobby, you know as well as anyone that we live in an outrage culture. Everybody's always mad about something, especially on the Internet. Just give it twenty-four hours and everybody will go back to arguing what color a shoe is or who has the best chicken sandwich."

"It's not like that this time," Besserman said. "You grew up in Texas. You know what a ranch is like. Everybody loves a juicy steak or a good hamburger until they see how the meat is acquired. Intelligence is a messy business, and when our unmentionables get put on full display, we have to deal with this kind of blowback. And unfortunately, it's not something we can just wish away."

Blunt smiled as a thought occurred to him. "Then let's not wish it away, Bobby. Let's turn the tables on these criminals masquerading as public servants in the halls of congress and on our military bases abroad."

"That's easier said than done."

"Nonsense," Blunt said. "Public opinion can turn on a dime, and if we have the kind of information that will expose Gaither, let's do it."

"And how do you suggest we do that?"

"You're not gonna like this idea."

"Try me."

Blunt sighed. "Wikileaks."

"No, absolutely not," Besserman said. "You know we can't do that, not after what happened the last time."

"It gives us a way to flip public sentiment almost instantaneously."

"And you're certain what's contained on those files will do that?"

"At this point, it's all we've got. Can I count on you to do that?"

"I'll consider it, but I'm not making any promises."

Blunt hung up and transmitted the files to Besserman. The Firestorm director knew a human trafficking ring would get the public to light its pitch forks. But that couldn't have been all. And if Gaither was willing to kill for what was on that file, Blunt figured it had to be even more damning—if that was even possible.

A half-hour later, Blunt's phone rang with an incoming call, the identity of the caller shielded.

"Senator Blunt, this is the office of the President of the United States," a pleasant woman said. "Please stay on the line for the president."

Moments later, Conrad Michaels's voice boomed from the other end. "J.D., how are ya today?"

"I'd be a lot better if I could get a full night of sleep every now and then."

Michaels chuckled. "What's keeping you up at night? The Astros' bullpen?"

"I have more confidence in them than I do the Nationals' relievers. That's a disaster waiting to happen around the seventh inning every night."

"If only I could justify applying some of the country's defense budget to help the Nationals protect a late-inning lead."

Blunt laughed. "Well, I'm sure you didn't call me this early to talk baseball, did you, sir?"

"Always straight to the point. That's why I like you so much, J.D. Well, the reason I'm calling is to issue a personal invitation to you for the awards ceremony tonight at the Kennedy Center. I'd really love for you to join us. I even have a seat for you in a private box with Katherine Thornhill, the lovely congresswoman from Oklahoma."

"Mr. President, are you really trying to play matchmaker with me tonight? I mean, I'm flattered that you would think of me and use your power to pull a few strings, but you know I'm perfectly content living as a single man since Vivian passed away."

"That's what they all say, but I know better than that. You need a good woman, and Katherine's one of the best out there."

"I appreciate that, sir. But I'm too old to get remarried."

"That's the most ridiculous thing I've ever heard. You're barely sixty-five years old and can still get around just fine."

Blunt laughed. "Sir, I use a cane."

"Look, we're on a secure line, so you don't have to play games with me. I know that is actually a weapon and you can still run with the best of them. Your act might not be evident to everyone, but I've known you for too long."

"Okay, okay," Blunt said with a chuckle. "I'll be there. But I'm not coming for her. I'm coming to support you. Just make sure Nate Miller doesn't see me because I don't want to end up in *The Post's* "Washington Whispers" column about my budding romance with Katherine Thornhill."

"Oh, I'm sorry, J.D. You didn't hear?"

"Hear what?"

"About Nate Miller. It was all on the news this morning."

"What happened to him?" Blunt asked.

"He was found dead last night from a heart attack."

"A heart attack? That's preposterous."

"The report I heard said that he had complained about some chest pain earlier in the day, and he'd been in the hospital a few months ago for similar symptoms."

"I'm not buying that," Blunt said. "That's just too strange, especially after he broke that story about the stranded pilot in Russia."

"Maybe," Michaels said. "I don't know. I think it's easy to see a conspiracy when we want to. It makes us think that there has to be some reason for it all as opposed to just the heartbreaking side of life."

"He was murdered," Blunt said emphatically. "I'd bet my own life on it."

"It's unfortunate that he's gone. However, I can't promise that someone else won't be there to report that you and Katherine Thornhill were canoodling in a private box at the Kennedy Center."

"That's because we won't be," Blunt said. "I'm only coming to support you, sir. And don't get any other ideas about it."

Michaels chuckled. "Great. I look forward to seeing you tonight. Oh, and one more thing."

"What's that, sir?"

"I'm sure you've heard that every agency in the city is looking for Titus Black."

"Yes, I'm aware of that situation."

"I know you were friends with his father, so you haven't happened to have heard from him, have you?"

Blunt paced around his office. "Why would you

think he'd try to reach out to me?"

"I don't know. Just playing a hunch."

"I haven't spoken to him in quite a while," Blunt said, selling the lie with all the sincerity he could muster.

"Well, please help us if you do. That bastard needs to pay for what he did."

"*If* he did what they're accusing him of," Blunt corrected.

"Why would you think otherwise? He's the reason my son is dead. That bastard never answered for that."

"I believe he was exonerated by an investigation, wasn't he?"

Michaels grunted. "Don't be ridiculous, J.D. You've been in this city long enough to know that exoneration isn't the same as a declaration of innocence."

"Perhaps you're right, but I'd suggest trying not to let that cloud your judgment."

"How can I not? Michael Jr.'s absence is a daily reminder of how Titus Black failed me and this country."

"I understand how you feel, sir. I trust we'll be able to find him soon and get the answers we all want."

Blunt hung up and slung his phone across the

room. He had been friends with President Michaels for a long time, but he was still blaming the loss of his son on Black. And Michaels seemed intent on exacting some sort of revenge on Black.

Blunt was convinced more than ever that Senator Gaither knew precisely how to manipulate the situation to get away with his crime. And the Firestorm director was determined more than ever not to let that happen.

He slumped into his chair and stared out the window as the sun rose over the Potomac. He knew there wasn't much time left for Titus Black to prove who was really behind the shooting and what it was all about.

CHAPTER 30

BLACK SPENT THE MORNING sifting through all the files that Shields had managed to decrypt, which weren't many. They were mostly more emails between the Russian general, Ivan Kozlov, all discussing dates and times for pickups for certain "packages."

"These would be enough to turn public sentiment," Black said, "but we need more than that right now."

"I'm starting to worry that there isn't a smoking gun in here," Shields said.

"Do you need another energy drink?" Black asked.

"Of course, but I'm not about to let you go outside and get one for me. And the fridge is bare."

Black sighed and paced around the room. "What are we missing? There's got to be something else here."

By lunchtime, Black was starting to wonder if he should resign himself to his fate. He couldn't live holed up in a safe house his whole life. Not that he would survive in such confined quarters anyway. He needed wide open spaces, the smell of pine trees while hiking up a mountainside, the crisp sound of frost crunching beneath his feet on a late fall morning. Hiding from the FBI and every other agency hunting for him sounded about the same as prison. It sounded like his personal version of hell.

"Cheer up," Shields said. "We're going to find something. I just know it."

"I'm glad you have confidence in yourself," Black said. "It's a good trait to have."

"You have it too."

"Unfortunately, not in this case. I'm used to everyone letting me down, remember?"

"Your stepdad?"

Black nodded. "And the Air Force, which didn't act fast enough to get my father when he was shot down while flying his A-10 over Afghanistan."

"That's why you didn't hesitate to go after Captain Watkins, isn't it? You wanted to do for him what no one did for your dad, didn't you?"

"And I rescued him only to drag him back here and put him right in the center of the bullseye for someone within his own government," Black said. "Some messiah I was for Watkins."

"Sometimes you can do everything right and it

still goes wrong. It's not your fault what happened to him here."

"But I could have prevented it. He was scared—and for good reason, too. I should've listened to him and taken his concerns more seriously. That's why I think there's got to be more to this than what we're seeing on the surface."

"Then let's dig deeper. Talking about it isn't going to help us rectify this situation."

"Just play along with me for a second here," Black said. "I'm spitballing, but I think we need to consider why Gaither and his cohorts would try to murder me."

"It's pretty simple—you know the truth."

Black wagged his index finger at her. "I'm not so sure that's the only reason."

"With Watkins gone, you're the only person who could implicate them at this point in this ring. There's no other evidence."

"But my evidence is only hearsay, according to the courts. It'd just be what I learned in a conversation I had with Watkins. And you and I both know that kind of shaky evidence could get tossed out easily by a judge, especially a judge who owes Senator Gaither a few favors."

"You did have the flash drive. Maybe that's what they were really after."

Black shrugged. "Great. So, the answer to why Gaither's men want me dead is on an encrypted file that not even our own NSA can crack."

"Hasn't cracked yet," Shields corrected. "Gotta think positive here."

"I'll keep my fingers crossed, but I'm not counting on anybody coming through for us."

"Look, just because you've been let down in the past doesn't mean you should stop trusting people all the time everywhere, much less counting on them. I know in the world of espionage, trust is viewed as a negative characteristic, but it can turn out to be a positive one. *Trust me.*"

She winked at Black.

Black rolled his eyes. "That was a great pep talk, right up until the moment that you decided that lame joke was necessary."

"Get over here and help me look at this from a fresh perspective," she said. "I've been staring at the screen longer than you have. Maybe I'm missing something."

Then Shields's phone rang with a call from Blunt. She put the call on speaker.

"Please tell me the NSA came through," she said.

"Mallory Kauffman, to be exact," Blunt said. "Ever heard of her?"

"I've heard her name."

"She's the analyst Besserman assigned to help with this project. And it so happens that she and I have a mutual acquaintance. She just sent back the files she was able to crack. I made a copy and will try to see what I can find, but I know you're the best one qualified for the job."

"What did she say about what she found?" Shields asked.

"Nothing, just that it still seemed like the messages were written in some kind of code. She said she'd make another run at them later but had a more pressing matter on her plate."

"We'll call you if we find something," she said.

"Good luck," Blunt said before he hung up.

Energized by the prospect of looking at something different, Black pulled up a chair next to Shields as the two agents sifted through the new emails that had previously been secure. But by the time 4:00 p.m. rolled around, they still hadn't found anything substantive.

"This isn't getting us anywhere," Black said. "I have no idea why these files were even secured in the first place. There's nothing here."

"The only thing that looks odd to me is all these numbers appear to be randomly dropped into their conversations," Shields said. "Look at this one."

Black jotted down the numbers, and his eyes

widened. "This is today's date."

"And look what else appears in this message," she said, pointing at the screen.

"Gaither was feeding information to Roman, who was passing it along to Kozlov," Black said. "And then there's Michaels's name. They're going to try and assassinate Michaels."

"But why? What would Gaither have to gain from eliminating the president?"

Black shrugged. "I'm not sure, but it's spelled out in black and white for us right here."

"See if you can reach Blunt. Maybe he can alert the Secret Service about the threat."

Black dialed Blunt's number. The call went straight to voicemail. After a couple minutes, Black entered the number before Shields stopped him from calling again.

"Leave it alone," she said. "Someone might be monitoring his phone. We don't want to risk having our location exposed."

"But we have to tell Secret Service. Somebody needs to know before they arrive at the Kennedy Center."

"That's not our job, especially when you're being hunted."

"You're right," Black said. "It's not our job. It's our duty. If some foreign government is on our soil and has a plot to assassinate our president, we need to do something about it."

"What are you gonna do? Go down there?"

"That's exactly what I plan on doing," Black said.

"You'll never get close enough to Michaels," she said. "And if you do, who knows if he'll even listen to you. He still blames you for what happened to his son."

"It might be the only way out of my current situation. If I save President Michaels, it'll prove where my loyalties lie. No one will believe that I was trying to kill Gaither, especially after we expose him for what he truly is: a traitor."

"You're right," she said, "but I still don't think you need to go charging into the lion's den while that target is painted on your chest."

"If I can get behind enemy lines in Russia, I can get behind enemy lines in my own country," Black said.

"But you don't even know how the Russians plan on killing Michaels tonight."

"Right now, that's the least of my concerns," Black said. "I've got to figure out a way inside first. After that, I'll worry about the rest."

"For the record, I don't like this," Shields said.

"Well, I'm not doing this alone," he said. "Without you, none of this is going to work. So, are you in?"

Shields nodded resolutely. "Of course. I'll follow you and keep you off the security cameras with a little bit of my wizardry."

"A little bit of your magic always helps," he said as he grabbed his keys and darted toward the door.

CHAPTER 31

BLUNT LUMBERED UP THE STEPS to the president's private box and steadied himself with his cane before easing into his chair. The auditorium was teeming with security, a sure sign that the president would appear soon.

While the crowd filed into their seats, Blunt leaned forward and scanned the sea of people below him. He spotted a handful of the city's most well-known lobbyists as well as a few other high-ranking officials from both political parties, all eager to be seen at the prestigious Kennedy Center Honors ceremony. If there was one thing that could unite Washington, it was a celebration of the performing arts. Several dignitaries from other countries were filling up their boxes on the mezzanine level, giving the event a decidedly global flavor to it. And based on the award recipients, that made sense.

The most famous of all the actors and singers was Anna Tara, the latest starlet to dazzle Hollywood.

Her movies had become some of the highest grossing dramas in the movie industry over the past several years, making her one of the most sought-after actresses. But her friendly disposition and warm personality made her a hit among fans, who she embraced no matter where she was or what she was doing.

Blunt had seen a couple of her films and was impressed. He was also interested where she came from since she seemed to emerge out of nowhere to become a hot commodity in a business where most people are forced to pay their dues before winning any major roles. What he found was that she didn't just stumble into her stardom. For several years, she had been paying her dues in the fledgling Ukranian movie market, making films under her given name, Anastasia Tarasenko. She assumed a more westernized version of her name at the behest of her agent when she first auditioned for a role in a movie produced in Hollywood. And everything was launched from there.

Out of the corner of his eye, Blunt noticed someone easing into the seat to his right.

"Ms. Thornhill," Blunt said as he turned and offered his hand.

She smiled as she settled into her chair. "I must be in the wrong box."

"I know," Blunt said. "How you got stuck with

the commoners is something I'd take up with management here."

She chuckled and waved dismissively. "I don't know if anyone has told you this, but I'm a sucker for flattery."

Blunt shrugged. "It's Washington. Isn't everyone?"

"Good point. We do love our egos stroked here, don't we?"

"Speaking of which, have you seen the president? I wanted to thank him for getting me into his private box, but I haven't seen hide nor hair of him."

"That's because he's only going to be in here for a few minutes. He wanted to participate in handing out the awards this year."

"Really?" Blunt said, furrowing his brow. "That doesn't sound like him."

"I think he wanted to meet Anna Tara from what I hear."

"Well, I think we'd all jump at the chance to shake her hand and have a picture taken with her. She's such a breath of fresh air among most of the Hollywood types."

"Absolutely," Thornhill said. "The president is going to hand out her award tonight with Vasyl Petrenko."

"Why would he share the stage with the Ukranian

president? That's an odd move sure to ruffle the Russian's feathers."

"*Designed* to ruffle feathers," she corrected. "Michaels knows what he's doing."

"And I'm not sure that's the brightest idea."

"If you feel strongly about it, perhaps you should return to the senate and do something."

Blunt sighed and shook his head. "My days at the Capitol building are long gone. I prefer to do most of my work out of the limelight."

"Well, I certainly rue the fact that I never got to work with you," she said. "I've heard great things about your statesmanship."

"Whoever told you such things didn't tell you the full story."

"Enlighten me."

"There's not much to it," Blunt said. "The truth is I discovered that being amenable to other's ideas that I didn't fully agree with just so I could get part of my agenda passed only watered down my influence. In my latter years, I found a much more direct approach worked better, enabling me to achieve more than I ever thought possible."

"That sounds like a ringing endorsement."

Blunt winked and nodded. "Just be sure that you're ready to leave your position when you do start behaving in such a manner. You won't be long for this city if you speak truthfully."

Before their conversation went any further, a strange hush fell over the auditorium as everyone started to pick up their phones. The eerie silence was followed by gasps and then a murmur that spread across the room like a wave. While many of the people in attendance just read the news with mouths agape, many political officials left their seats to answer calls or make them.

"I wonder what that's all about," Thornhill said.

"Perhaps you should look at your phone," Blunt said.

"I didn't bring it. I've found it ruins good conversation."

"Or it could be incited by your phone."

"I guess it all depends on your point of view," Thornhill said.

Blunt swiped on his phone's screen, revealing an alert from *The Washington Post* app. He feigned surprise, if only for Thornhill's benefit.

"What's it say?" she asked.

"See," Blunt said, shaking his phone. "This already has you interested—and I haven't even told you what I read."

"Okay, fine. Tell me what it says. The suspense is killing me."

"Wikileaks just released a cache of documents

detailing how Senator Gaither helped support a human trafficking ring with the help of some nefarious Air Force base commanders."

"Are you serious?"

"I wish I weren't," Blunt said. "If Gaither hasn't resigned by the end of the night, I'll be shocked."

"He's still in the hospital, isn't he?"

Blunt shrugged. "Does it matter? Seems like maybe there's more to that attempted assassination story than we thought."

"What do you mean?"

"Maybe the shooter was gunning for Captain Watkins and trying to make it appear as though Gaither was the target."

Thornhill's eyebrows shot upward. "That's a serious accusation, Mr. Blunt. Or is that based off more than just conjecture?"

"I'll let the suspense kill you slowly," he said with a wink.

The house lights blinked, signaling the event was about to begin.

"Have you seen the president?" Thornhill asked.

Blunt shook his head. "I've been looking for him ever since I walked in. There was something I wanted to tell him."

"Me, too," she said. "But apparently we're just guests in his box and not important enough to sit near him."

"It does look that way, doesn't it?"

Blunt's phone buzzed with a message from Shields. He picked up his cell and scanned the text.

Black is headed to the Kennedy Ctr to warn the prez … his life is in danger. Can you warn him first?

Blunt texted back that he'd try. He shoved his phone back into his pocket and glanced around. The president nor any of his Secret Service detail were anywhere to be seen.

Blunt got up and headed toward the box exit to see if he could find someone who could help. Right before he stepped into the hallway, a security guard stepped in front of Blunt and straddled the doorway. The man scowled and nodded in the direction of Blunt's chair.

"I need to make a phone call," Blunt said.

The guard didn't move and slowly placed his hands on his hips, peeling back his sports coat to reveal his sidearm piece. He cut his eyes toward it, sending a not-so-subtle message.

Blunt persisted. "It's really important," he said in a hushed tone.

The man leaned in. "If you make one move outside of this box, I'm going to usher you out permanently. Is that understood?"

Blunt spun around and took two steps toward his seat before whipping around and darting toward the exit. But the guard stepped in front and bear-hugged Blunt, wrapping him up and dragging him down the hall.

"The president is in danger," Blunt said. "I need to warn him."

"He's always in danger," the guard said with a sneer. "Now, let's get you outta here."

"You don't know who you're messing with," Blunt said as he kicked and squirmed in an effort to break free. But it was no use. The brute wasn't about to let anyone acting as crazy as Blunt was any distance down the hallway toward President Michaels's box.

"Someone's going to try and kill him tonight," Blunt said.

"Yeah, yeah, you crazy old man," the guard said. "Now why don't you do us all a favor and get in bed on time tonight, okay? And don't forget to take your meds when you wake up in the morning."

Blunt was already stewing over the fact that he couldn't speak with anyone in any meaningful position near the president. But then to be patronized by the thick-necked enforcer at the doorway? Blunt had little patience for such behavior, though there was nothing he could do about it in the moment.

And the moment of reckoning was fast approaching, faster than Blunt had hoped.

CHAPTER 32

Washington, D.C.

TATIANA TUGGED ON THE LACE encircling the waist of her leotard. She pulled it taut and took a deep breath. The girls all around her giggled nervously as they discussed their plans for later that evening. While the other dancers talked incessantly about everything from movies to boys they liked to school activities, Tatiana kept her distance. She didn't want to make any missteps, especially when she was so close to completing her assignment.

"Emily, where are you going afterward?" one of the girls asked. "Would you like to join us?"

Tatiana forced a smile. "No, thank you. I have a big day tomorrow."

"What are you doing?" another girl asked, leaning in as she awaited the answer.

Tatiana paused for a moment, pondering the quickest way to end the conversation without drawing more questions. "I have a science competition I'm going to."

"The one in New York?" the first girl asked.

Tatiana nodded. "I think so. My mom makes all the plans, and I just go where she tells me to go."

"I know that all too well," one of the dancers chimed in. "My mother just has me whisked around from one activity to the next by our poor chauffeur, Reginald. The man must enjoy that car because he's in it all day long."

The pretentious response ignited a short game of one-upmanship between a trio of the teenage performers. But Tatiana didn't mind, smiling as she eased into the shadows away from the prying eyes of the other dancers. She reached into her bag and took one last glance around before tucking the long knife up her sleeve.

Tatiana swallowed hard as she positioned the blade exactly as she'd practiced many times before for the general. Her ability to release and catch the knife in one fell swoop—all while driving the tip into a combatant's neck—was her specialty. And she couldn't wait to do it tonight for the first time. She felt an odd peace about completing the assignment. It was brutal in nature, a violent end to an operation that was mostly about getting into the right place at the right time. What she did after that was simple execution, though it'd be an actual execution that would likely be remembered in all the history books. At least, that's what the general had said.

Tatiana had trained long and hard, all with the understanding that she was going to do something great for her country. And when she did, she could go home.

But for the first time, Tatiana pondered the thought of what might happen if she didn't succeed.

A few minutes later, the instructor summoned the dancers. The girls remained offstage, running through the routine quickly before their scheduled appearance on the main stage.

As she prepared for her first grand jeté, one of the stagehands stopped Tatiana, pulling her out of the rhythm of the dance. She looked down at the man's hand, which had wrapped around her bicep and was squeezing her.

"Owww," Tatiana said, ripping her arm away from the man.

"I saw something glint off your sleeve," he said. "Show me your arm."

Tatiana smiled. "What are you talking about?"

He turned her right wrist over and snatched her sleeve back before releasing her. "I'm sorry, but I must've been mistaken."

Tatiana eased the blade into her left sleeve while

his eyes were focused on her right.

As she turned to walk away, he stopped her again. "No. Wait a minute." he said. "I still see something. Come here right now."

Tatiana walked over to him, feigning ignorance as much as possible and turning on her charm. "If you want my number, you can just ask for it," she said.

"Don't be so presumptuous," the man said. "You're not my type."

"So my age doesn't bother you?" Tatiana asked as she grabbed the man's shirt and tugged on it, pulling him closer to her. "What do you say?"

"What do *you* say you show me that thing tucked up your sleeves that's reflecting off the overhead lighting. We don't need anything like that occurring during the production."

"It's just your imagination," Tatiana said, holding out both arms as she backed into the shadows offstage. "There's nothing here. See?"

"I could've sworn I saw something there," he said, grabbing her wrist again.

"There was," Tatiana said as she released her knife and drove the blade up through the man's neck. Before his blood made a mess, she ripped open one of the prop chests and stuffed him inside. She was certain that nobody had seen her.

Tatiana wiped the knife clean, cleaning off the

blood on the man's pants. She noticed some blood trickling out of the corner near the base of the box. Grabbing a coat from the inside of the costume box, she used the piece of clothing to mop up the trickling blood before tossing it back inside.

Promptly re-securing the knife, she raced back out into the rehearsal room and picked up where she'd left off, performing her grand jeté as she leaped across the makeshift stage.

"Is everyone ready?" the instructor called, clapping her hands to signal for everyone to line up.

"The show just started," the woman said. "We're on in one hour."

In sixty minutes, she was going to end the president's life. And she couldn't wait to do it so she could go home.

CHAPTER 33

BLACK PARKED HIS CAR in the deck and eyed one of the catering vans loading up empty hors d'oeuvres trays and used glassware. He eased next to the vehicle and waited for the guy who appeared to be in his early twenties. Once he was by himself, Black whispered to get his attention.

"Hey, bud. Want to make a quick extra two hundred bucks?" Black asked, signaling for the guy to come closer.

The young man looked around before hustling over to Black. "Maybe. What do you need me to do?"

"I need you to take the night off and give me your catering jacket," Black said.

He was already wearing dark pants and only needed a white jacket—and a security clearance badge—to complete the look.

"Why not?" the guy said. "I was just filling in tonight for a friend anyway."

"Great," Black said. "Give me your coat there,

and I'll give you the money."

The two swapped items before Black rushed over to the door, keeping his head down as he meandered inside. He turned the corner and came face-to-face with a security guard checking all the passes. When he saw Black in a catering outfit, the man hardly looked at the badge and waved Black through the metal detector, which didn't go off.

Just as he was about to turn the corner, the guard called after Black. "Hey, you. Come here."

Black froze, unsure if he should run and verify his status as an intruder, which would also give him the best chance to get away, or politely return and see what the man wanted. As much as Black wanted to select the first option, he chose the second.

"What is it, sir?" Black asked in as polite of a manner as he could muster.

"Do you guys still have any of those little hotdog thingys that you pick up with a toothpick?"

"Are you talking about Little Smokies?"

"Sure," the guy said. "I don't know. Whatever you call them. Just bring me a small plate of them if you don't mind. My stomach is about to eat itself I'm so hungry."

Black nodded. "Of course. I'll be back in a jiffy with a plate of Little Smokies just for you."

Relieved that the summons was nothing more

than that, Black hustled down the hallway before taking a hard right once he glanced over his shoulder and had noticed that the guard had returned to reading his magazine.

"I'm in," Black said after he turned on his coms and affixed it to his ear.

"Took you long enough," Shields said. "And now you need to hurry."

Black shed his jacket to reveal his tuxedo as he ascended the steps and arrived on the main floor. He needed to warn the president about the imminent danger, but Black had a plethora of obstacles to overcome, starting with access.

The steps to the balcony were reserved for VIPs with a special access badge. Black didn't have one, nor did he want to get too close to anyone for fear that they might recognize him. The initial images of Black plastered on television looked nothing like him, but according to Shields, the latest reports revealed Black in his most recent hairstyle and color.

"Don't get too close," Shields said. "I'm sure that Gaither alerted the FBI and the Secret Service about what you look like now. And agents from both those agencies will be looking for you, trying to keep you as far away from the president as possible, most likely by taking you into custody."

"So, what am I supposed to do?" he asked.

"Why are you asking me? You're the one who said you'd figure it out when you got there."

Black strode toward a fire alarm.

"Don't even think about it," she said. "That will only create more chaos and be far more difficult to control."

"But it gives me an advantage since I can charge headlong into the crowd streaming toward the exits without anyone paying me any attention."

"Titus Ulysses Black, you turn around right now," she said.

"You're watching me, aren't you?" he asked.

"Like a hawk."

"Okay, instead of chastising all my ideas, can you possibly think of one yourself and pass it along? I'm starting to get desperate."

"I tapped into the Kennedy Center's security network, and I'm scanning the footage as we speak," Shields said.

"Again, that doesn't do me any good."

"Of course it does when I can transmit this to your phone so you can see what I'm looking at," she said.

Black's phone buzzed with a message from Shields that was a simple link.

"I'm assuming you want me to click on this, unless you've decided to Rick Roll me at one of the worst times ever."

Shields chuckled. "Select the app I just sent you, and that should be able to see everything I can."

"What good is this going to do me if I can't get inside the auditorium?"

"Just check out the still photography I added to that email and let me know what you think."

"I'm not sure I can see everyone distinctly," she said.

"Me either," Black said. "But it'll have to do."

"Why don't you use the back stairwell and find a spot where you can assess the audience and possible attack points in the building."

"Roger that," Black said.

He entered a side door and started climbing the steps, two or three at a time. After he'd worked his way up two flights of stairs, he stopped. He wanted to wait for someone to exit through those doors as they inevitably do. But after five minutes of waiting, nobody came.

Frustrated, Black sat on the top step just below the landing and watched Shields's cameras roam back and forth across the room.

"There he is," Black said as he eased to his feet.

The door flung open, catching Black off guard. He put his head down as a familiar-looking man barely gave Black a second glance.

Black hopped to his feet and then grabbed the

handle just before the door closed. He glanced behind him once more when he heard heavy footfalls approaching his position. Without hesitating, Black darted down the hallway and then ducked into a closet.

"Shields, can you hear me?" Black asked.

"Loud and clear," she said. "Are you in some kind of trouble?"

"Just help me find a place where I can hide until he's gone."

"Hang on a sec," she said. "Let me pull up the schematics."

"Come on, come on," Black said. "I need to know where to go right now."

"Okay got it. Just up ahead, turn left. There's a service closet on the right."

Black followed Shields's instruction and slipped inside. For the first time in ten minutes, Black caught his breath—and he wondered if he'd be able to help the president before it was too late.

"What have you got, Shields?" he whispered.

"Well, you're not gonna like this—"

She finished her thought, but Black never heard it. The door to the closet flung open. And standing over him was a Secret Service agent.

"Well, well, well, if it isn't Washington's most famous fugitive," the man said, training his gun on Black.

"You're going to make a big mistake if you arrest me," Black said. "The president's life is in danger."

"Yeah, because of you," the agent said. "Now, hands where I can see them. Let's not make this any more difficult than it has to be."

Black held out his hands and shivered as the cold metal cuffs slid around his wrists.

CHAPTER 34

Washington, D.C.

SHIELDS WATCHED OVER the security cameras as Black was apprehended by the Secret Service agent. She felt helpless, unable to do anything about it. After slamming her fist onto her desk, she got up and paced around the room. Short of going to the Kennedy Center, she was running out of ideas. But even that was a long shot. By the time she got down there, it'd likely be too late.

She listened as the man who arrested Black called for assistance over his coms. Black sat down, leaning against the wall. She was tempted to say something, but she didn't want to risk her voice being heard and losing contact with him.

While she took in the scene on her monitor, her cell rang with a call from a number she didn't recognize.

"Christina Shields," she said as she answered.

"Yes, Ms. Shields," the caller said, "my name is Mallory Kauffman. I work with the NSA."

"Oh, yes. I'm familiar with who you are. I believe you were working on cracking some files for me."

"That's right. Well, I had some extra time tonight and started to look at those encrypted messages again. It seems like they were written in some sort of code."

"We were able to crack that. The Russians are planning to make an attempt on the life of the president tonight."

"Are you sure about that?" Kauffman asked. "Because there's more to this code."

"What do you mean?"

"Today's date is in the message as is President Michaels's name. But I don't think he's the target."

"Why not? Who else could they be after?" Shields asked.

"I found another name embedded in that same message, one you likely would've missed—Vasyl Petrenko."

"The Ukranian president?"

"Yeah, and he's at the Kennedy Center tonight too."

"Do you think Petrenko and Michaels are both being targeted?"

"I don't think the Russians are itching for a war with us, but I got an alert tonight on some unusual activity in the Russian region near Ukraine. According to some of the satellite imagery I was looking at, there's been quite a bit of action on the border as the Russians are amassing troops there as if they're about to invade. It's like sharks circling their prey."

"This is about that defense technology, isn't it?" Shields asked.

"Who knows what incited this. I don't think it takes much for either one of these countries to get angered by the other. They're both looking for a reason to go to war and settle their conflict. But one thing's for sure: if the Russians assassinate Petrenko tonight, full-fledged war will break out. That much is guaranteed."

"Just an attempt on Petrenko's life will do that."

"You're probably right."

"One of our agents went to the Kennedy Center to try and alert security there about the potential threat, but he's not having much luck at the moment. Have you let your boss know?"

"I tried," Kauffman said, "but he hasn't called me back yet. He's dealing with all the fallout from the Wikileaks information dump that just happened. Apparently, Senator Gaither is upset that his good name is being sullied."

"That should be the least of Gaither's concerns right now," Shields said.

"I'll keep trying with Besserman. And good luck with your operative."

Shields hung up and glanced back at the screen where the Secret Service agent had been holding Black. Her mouth fell agape.

The hallway was empty.

She clicked furiously through all the cameras, searching for Black to learn where he was or where he had been taken.

But he wasn't anywhere to be seen.

Shields took a deep breath and then tried to raise him on the coms. "I've lost visual with you, Black," she said in a hushed tone. "But I need to know you can hear me. Just say something to let me know you're okay and maybe a clue as to where you are."

She waited and waited. He didn't reply.

CHAPTER 35

BLACK PUT HIS HEAD DOWN and removed the ear piece in an effort to make sure if Shields said anything, it wouldn't further complicate the situation. With no voices in his head, he pondered a path out of his current situation. Every second that passed meant the president was that much closer to being murdered in the most public of ways. And Black couldn't stand to sit around any longer and wait for another Secret Service agent to explain the situation to. There wasn't any guarantee that he would listen either.

Black looked up at the man. "Listen here, Agent—"

"Edgerton."

"Agent Edgerton, I know you think you're doing some great service for your country, but the reality is that you are going to be the reason the president ends up dead if you don't let me go."

"This is rich coming from a trained assassin who's running around taking out high-ranking politicians."

Black shook his head slowly. "You have no idea what you're talking about. I would never do anything to compromise this country's security."

"What do you think attempted murder on a sitting senator qualifies as? Keeping our country safe?"

"Keep talking," Black said. "You're only showing your ignorance. And by the time one of your superiors decides to come up here, the president will be dead."

The agent set his jaw. "Did you plant a bomb here?"

"You're really not listening to me, are you?" Black said. "There's an active threat in the building—and it's not me."

"Oh, I hear you, but I don't believe you."

"Then your principled stand here will betray your oath to protect the Commander in Chief."

The agent huffed a laugh through his nose. "Just for fun, let's say I let you go. What would you do? Run on stage with President Michaels while he and Petrenko are draping a sash over Anna Tara."

"If that's what it takes, yes. I don't know if you're being this obtuse on purpose, but you're going to regret all this mockery if you don't let me go do what I came here to do."

"You can stop talking now because I'm not buying what you're selling."

Black put his head down and contemplated his

next decision. He needed to move quick before more of the agent's colleagues joined him.

"Look, I'll make a deal with you. You let me go, and I won't hurt you."

The man chuckled and shook his head. "The report on you said you were arrogant. It wasn't a joke."

"And if you don't want to be the punchline, just release me and I'll forget the whole thing ever happened."

"I think you've forgotten who's holding the gun."

Black didn't look up at the man, who was just out of arm's length. Instead, Black sprang into action from the most unassuming position, catching the agent off guard.

Black thrust his leg out, connecting with the man's knee cap as he crumpled to the floor in pain. He tried to maintain his grip on his weapon but couldn't due to the pain in his leg. Black kicked it aside. When the agent attempted to activate his coms and notify his fellow Secret Service members that he was under attack, Black stomped on his hand and then ripped out the coms cord and tossed it away.

The agent scratched and clawed at the floor, trying to drag his lame body toward the weapon. Black slid the gun aside with his foot before straddling the man from behind and putting him in a sleeper hold. After a brief struggle, he fell limp.

Black dragged the man into the closet and took off his jacket and pants. They weren't a perfect fit, but it was close enough. The agent's gun, however, fit perfectly in the palm of Black's hand.

While the weapon was a much-needed accessory, Black was most interested if he could pass for being a member of the Secret Service without getting called out. He slipped in the man's coms and listened for any chatter. For the moment, everything was silent.

Black then re-inserted his other ear piece so he could talk with Shields.

"Shields, are you there? Do you copy?" he asked as he hustled toward a back stairwell that led to the catwalk.

After a brief pause, her voice came through loud and clear. "I'm here," she said. "What happened to you? I was watching you one minute, and the next you were gone."

"I had to subdue my new Secret Service friend and secure him. Once I did that, I swapped clothes with him, and I'm now heading to the catwalk to see if I can get a better view of what's happening."

"Ah, there you are," she said. "I'm looking at you now on the security cameras and it doesn't appear that anyone is heading toward your position—or where you were apprehended."

"Finally, some good news."

"Now there are a couple of things I need to tell you," she said.

"What is it?"

"We don't think Michaels is the target any more."

"What do you mean Michaels isn't the target?" Black asked, his mouth falling agape. "Who else could they be after?"

"Our friend over at the NSA found another name in that message—Vasyl Petrenko."

"The Ukranian president?"

"That's the one."

Black's eyes widened as he stopped. "He's going to be on stage with Michaels. The Secret Service agent mentioned something about Michaels and Petrenko being up there together when Anna Tara receives her award."

"Talk about a prime opportunity," Shields said. "One of the biggest stars in Hollywood standing next to the president when they try to assassinate Petrenko."

"So, do you still have eyes on the guy I was trying to tell you about before the meathead detained me?"

"That's the bad news. He got up and moved. And I can't find him anywhere."

"I'll see if I can get a bead on him from up here."

Black entered the catwalk encircling the auditorium high overhead. He peered into the sea of people below.

"I ran facial recognition on the guy you thought you recognized," Shields said. "His name is Yuri Smolov, and he's an operative with SVR, the Russian's foreign intelligence agency."

"He's the guy who tried to kill me at Union Station that day," Black said.

"That confirms that Gaither wasn't just ferrying around young girls in a human trafficking ring. He was bringing spies into the country."

"I wonder if Col. Roman knew anything about that."

"Hard to say at this point, but the picture is starting to become clearer and clearer as we dive deeper and deeper into this dark and twisted plot to kill . . . someone."

Black scanned the crowd below, focusing his search for a man in a navy blazer and a white shirt with a red tie. It didn't take long for Black to zero in on his suspect.

"Got him," Black said. "He's just to the right of the stage on the first row. It's easy access to the front."

"He's also got something in his pocket that he keeps fidgeting with," Shields said.

"Probably his gun. Keep an eye on him while I hustle downstairs. If he so much as sneezes, let me know immediately."

"What are you thinking?"

Black explained his plan briefly before he took off running.

"You better hurry," Shields said. "Anna Tara is about to step onto stage to accept her award. There's one more tribute before she does."

"I'll be there in time," he said. "You be ready when I give you the word."

CHAPTER 36

TATIANA SWALLOWED HARD as she pranced out onto the stage in formation with the rest of the dancers. Once she was in position, the music struck up and she twirled around, gracefully leaping and spinning with the dance troop. While the crowd wasn't there to see her play soccer, the high she got from performing as a dancer was just the same. She had always loved to dance yet found the discipline required to reach the pinnacle of the performance world far more strenuous than she wanted. At least as an athlete, the precision was as important while the taskmasters far less grueling.

The general was a collection of both the best and the worst. He had been encouraging when she was struggling, demanding when she wasn't. However, he held a high standard for everyone. And there was little room for errors. One mistake and he would send you to bed without any supper or take away your free time on Sunday afternoons. And while Tatiana wished for another life, she had grown to accept it—and at a much faster rate than her fellow recruits. It's why she was here, in this moment, on this stage.

As the movement slowed, Tatiana froze in position and scanned the eyes of the audience below. She wanted to see if her performance was delighting the crowd or simply passing the time until the real star graced the building with her presence. Despite her desire to assess the success of the dance based off the reaction from everyone in attendance, she couldn't see much past the fifth row. The faces of any people beyond that were difficult to see due to the bright lights beaming down across the stage.

Wearing a wide smile on her face, she scanned the gala attendees who were visible. They looked on in wide-eyed wonder as Valerie Gordon flew across the stage in the solo portion of the dance. Valerie was the star of the show, a "generational talent" Tatiana had heard one instructor call the dancer. And all eyes were glued to her as she seemed to float across the room with minimal effort. All eyes except for a pair belonging to one man on the front row. He wasn't watching Valerie; he was watching Tatiana.

Tatiana forced the wide smile across her face even as she found herself with shortness of breath.

What is Papa doing here? How did he know I would be here?

Her father looked at her and shook his head subtly.

Is he trying to tell me something? No? What's no?

For a fleeting moment, she considered the possibilities. How would he even know what she was doing here or what she was about to do?

Just over two years had passed since she last saw her father, since she last heard him answer the phone and then remain silent, unwilling to utter any response. But there he was, staring at her with the same type of intensity a surgeon does as he cuts out a brain tumor. The look he gave her wasn't warm or endearing. It was businesslike, and he clearly didn't want her doing what she was about to do.

He should've said something then. It's too late now. I'm going to do this for my country and to make the general proud.

As Valerie's solo concluded and she returned to formation with the rest of the dancers, Tatiana began twirling in synch with everyone else. They crisscrossed in the center of the stage, leaping between one another in a choreographed segment where the ballerinas appeared endlessly. Rotating around and around, the girls created a beautiful scene with their symmetry.

Tatiana had to make herself smile for most of the event, but not this time. Her grin was genuine, her pride swelling as she was just seconds away from completing her mission and getting to go home for good. The general had told her that someone would be there to pick her up and whisk her away once she completed her task. Perhaps it was her father. But she wasn't going to worry about that just yet. There was still work to be done, a president to kill.

Out of the corner of her eye, she noticed Anna Tara descending the steps, flanked by President Michaels and Vasyl Petrenko, President of Ukraine.

Perfect.

She made one last pass across the floor before turning near the corner and dancing straight toward Petrenko. The music faded away, and the crowd erupted in applause. Even Tatiana's father clapped. With his jaw set, he glared at her and subtly shook his head again. That wasn't the first time she'd seen that look from him, but it had been a long time. And she wasn't about to abandon everything she'd been training for over the past two years just because her father shook his head.

No, I'm going to make him proud.

Tatiana turned her back on the audience for the final time as she followed her fellow dancers in the exit pattern off the stage. Her target stood at the edge of her prescribed route, an arm's length distance away, close enough for her to strike in a manner so elegant people likely wouldn't realize what was happening.

As she moved within five meters of the trio of celebrities about to stride onto the stage, Tatiana released the knife, allowing it to fall right into her hand. She'd practiced the skilled move thousands of times before, and it all paid off as she prepared to drive the tip of the blade into Petrenko's neck.

Three, two, one . . .

The entire auditorium went dark and Tatiana stumbled around, unsure where exactly her target had gone.

CHAPTER 37

BLACK STOOD AT THE EDGE of the stage and watched Yuri Smolov closely as a ballet troop danced to the audience's delight. At different moments during the performance, he appeared to be communicating with someone through subtle movements. And Black wasn't about to let the Russian operative finish his assignment.

"Do it now," Black said.

The entire auditorium fell dark on his command.

"You've got fifteen seconds before the generators bring the house lights back," Shields said.

Black climbed onto the stage and raced toward the position he'd last seen President Michaels and Petrenko standing near Anna Tara. He jerked the two men's arms, pulling them toward the secret exit. As they all stumbled forward in the dark, Black led them to a stairwell and dragged them down two flights before arriving in a stark concrete room. He shoved them against the far wall just as the lights turned back on.

"Titus Black," Michaels said as he glared at his abductor. "I should've known."

"You should've known what, sir?" Black asked. "That I was going to save you from an assassination attempt."

"There are other people who are paid to protect me," Michaels said as he sneered at Black.

"And they wouldn't listen to me when I warned them that your life and the life of President Petrenko were in danger."

"In danger from who?" Michaels asked.

"The Russians."

"You mean to tell me that the Russians want to kill me and start another world war?"

Black shook his head. "They wanted to kill Petrenko, but if you were collateral damage, so be it."

"How dare you embarrass me like that," Petrenko said. "I get intelligence briefings every day, and there were never any threats mentioned like that."

"I apologize, Mr. President," Black said as he locked eyes with Petrenko. "Right now, the Russian army is gathering along the border, some fifty miles north of Kharkiv. As soon as you were killed, the plan was undoubtedly to invade during the chaos. But I just ruined their plans."

"This is absurd," Michaels said. "You're just botching another assignment again, aren't you?"

"Unless you consider botching a synonym for saving lives, then yes," Black said. "Otherwise, you're so wrong in your assessment of the situation that I can't even begin to address the number of issues with your statement."

"My son is dead because of you and—"

"Mr. President, that was a long time ago, and you don't know the whole story."

"I don't have to," Michaels said with a snarl. "You disregarded orders, and my son's entire life was gone in an instant. Had you followed protocol and listened to your superiors . . ."

"Probably many more people would be dead," Black said. "I'm truly sorry about what happened with your son, but that wasn't my fault. I wasn't the one who killed him."

Michaels glared at Black. "But he'd still be alive if you hadn't tried to intervene."

"I do have a few regrets in my life, Mr. President, but that's not one of them. I'm certain that more innocent lives would've been lost that day had I not done what I did. And while I'm sorry it was your son who paid the ultimate price, I was left with no choice. Your private grief versus the public grief of thousands? What would you do?"

Michaels screamed as he sprinted toward Black, who slid to the side and avoided a direct blow. The president glanced off Black and crumpled to the ground. A few seconds later, Michaels broke into tears, sobbing as he remained lying down.

Petrenko looked at the two men and hesitated, unsure of what to do.

Black nodded toward Michaels, giving the Ukranian permission to kneel next to his U.S. counterpart.

Meanwhile, footfalls on the steps outside arrested Black's attention. He raced to the door and spun around to face the two leaders he'd swept off the Kennedy Center stage.

"Whatever you do, don't leave this room until you hear from me," Black said. "I don't know how safe it is out there, but I do know that in the audience tonight there was at least one Russian—and I can promise you that he wasn't here to watch the ballet."

Michaels rolled over and sat up. He was still seething, wincing in pain as he moved.

"They're going to kill us, aren't they?" he asked.

Black shook his head. "Not if I can help it. Now stay put if you want to stay alive."

Hustling into the hallway, Black checked several nearby doors and found one that was unlocked. He opened it and crept into what was a large storage room. While the room was barely lit by the ambient light outside, he estimated it to stretch at least fifty meters deep and around thirty meters wide. A shelving system packed with props was arranged neatly for as far as he could see. Backdrops and scene scrims crowded against all four walls.

Black identified a position near the back that provided him with cover as well as a clean shot of the entrance. He crouched low and waited for the sound of anyone venturing toward him. It took less than a minute before Yuri Smolov approached the doorway.

He eased his hat into the opening. On the wall behind him, a perfect silhouette was cast, triggering Black to squeeze off a couple rounds. He blasted the hat, sending it flying in the air.

"Bravo, Mr. Black," Smolov said, his Russian accent strong. "You just wasted two shots. What do you think is going to happen when I have more shots than you do?"

Black snatched a football off a nearby shelf and launched the pigskin at the Russian spy. But instead of getting a snarky reply, Black watched Smolov somersault into the room before scrambling behind a crate in the corner nearest to the door.

Needing to draw Smolov's fire, Black located a prop leaning against the wall. It was the silhouette of a man, the wooden base attached to a set of wheels. Black gave it a shove, sending it flying out into the middle of the room. Smolov sat up and fired three shots at the board before figuring out it wasn't Black.

"You're one shot behind," Black said. "What's going to happen when you run out?"

For the next couple minutes, the two men traded shots. Black was convinced he could take out Smolov in the shadows, but that task proved more difficult than the Firestorm operative ever imagined possible.

Eventually, by Black's count, he had the lone remaining bullet.

"You think you're just going to walk up and shoot me?" Smolov said after a moment of silence. "What if I have another magazine ready to reload?"

"If that were true, you wouldn't be cowering behind some boxes."

"Mr. Black, do you know how much time SVR training concentrates on the art of throwing a knife?"

Black wasn't interested in having a conversation. He only wanted to drag Smolov's body onto the Kennedy Center stage to exonerate himself. It would be showy and probably a scene that would live forever on the Internet, but Black didn't care. He just wanted to prove wrong everyone who doubted his innocence.

Just as Black wondered if this fight was going to devolve into a standoff, he watched Smolov dart out of the room. Black chased after the Russian and took the final shot when he tried to unlock the door at the end of the hall.

The shot coerced Smolov to dive to the ground. Seconds later, he stood with bravado and glared at Black.

"They're in here, aren't they?" Smolov said, as much telling as he was asking. He took a few steps back and kicked down the door. He'd barely made it inside before Black leaped onto the Russian from behind, sending both men crashing to the floor.

Black stole a peek at the two presidents as they huddled in the corner.

"Get outta here, Mr. President," Black said. "You especially, President Petrenko."

But neither man moved, both apparently mesmerized by the fight unfolding in front of them, both likely scared they might be attacked on their way out of the room.

"Go now," Black urged again.

Just as Petrenko made a move toward the exit, Smolov lunged toward the Ukranian leader with a knife. Petrenko jumped back, narrowly avoiding a swipe from the blade.

"I'll finish you in a minute," Smolov said, sneering at Petrenko.

Black called Smolov, motioning for him to fight. "Leave the unarmed alone. Come fight a real man."

Smolov's nostrils flared as he glowered at Black. "You Americans always go sticking your nose where it doesn't belong."

Black edged closer to the Russian and ignored the comment. When Black feigned a lunge forward, Smolov drew back, making the mistake of leaving his hand exposed. Pouncing on the opportunity, Black kicked Smolov's hand and knocked the knife free. It clattered on the ground, skidding into the corner behind Smolov.

He glanced at the blade over his shoulder and walked backward toward it. As he bent down to pick it up, Black broke into an all-out sprint. He pinned Smolov against the wall behind him, preventing him from reaching the handle. Smolov writhed in an attempt to escape, twisting and turning but to no avail.

Black flipped Smolov over and put him in a sleeper hold.

With the threat momentarily secured, Black scrambled to his feet and started to search for something to tie up Smolov's hands and feet before calling the authorities and reporting the events that had unfolded.

"Finally," Black said with a sigh as he looked at Michaels, "we'll get some answers about what was really going on and who was involved."

But Black didn't see Petrenko, who had scooped the knife up off the ground. By the time Black turned around, Petrenko was savagely attacking the Russian spy. Black tried to stop the Ukrainian president, but he wasn't interested in interrogating the SVR agent.

After thirty seconds, Black pleaded with Petrenko to stop. "It's over, sir. He's not coming back to life. You've made sure of that."

Black glanced down at the concrete floor and noticed a thick stream of blood rapidly approaching his hand.

"Vasyl, why did you do that?" Michaels asked. "He's so much more valuable to us alive than dead."

"The only good Russian is a dead Russian," Petrenko said. "Besides, I'd never believe a word out of his mouth anyway."

Down the hall, the sound of boots stormed toward them. While Black was dreading that thunderous noise just a half-hour earlier, he welcomed it now. He wouldn't have to fight any more. It was over.

"Mr. President, are you all right?" one of the Secret Service agents asked as he entered the room.

He glanced at Petrenko. "I am now, thanks to my friend, President Petrenko. He killed one attacker and staved off another with a knife."

The agent shot a quick look at Black. "What do you want us to do with Mr. Black? I'm sure you're aware that he's a fugitive."

Michaels nodded. "Arrest him. This man tried to kill me. Hopefully he'll rot in prison for what he did."

"But Mr. President—" Black pleaded.

Michaels waved dismissively at Black then nodded knowingly at one of the Secret Service agents. The man grabbed Black and slapped a pair of handcuffs on him.

"You can't do this to me," Black said. "I just saved your life."

"No one will believe you, kid," Michaels said. "Thank goodness for Mr. Petrenko. Otherwise, we might all be dead except for you."

Black resisted the hands that clamped down on him, keeping him in place while the agents handcuffed him and escorted him toward the steps.

"You're making a mistake, you know," Black said as he walked away. "If I hadn't tried to warn you tonight about Yuri Smolov, you'd probably be dead right now."

Michaels didn't say a word, unwilling to even respond to Black's accusations.

"He's lying," Black said. "You gotta know that."

But the men who'd apprehended Black remained stoic, unmoved by his emotional pleas for help.

"Save it, pal," one of the men said. "They're going to put you in a hole. And you're going to stay there for a very long time."

CHAPTER 38

WHEN THE LIGHTS in the auditorium came back on, Tatiana was on stage, wielding her knife, searching in every direction for the two presidents who had vanished in the darkness. She turned to the left and then to the right, looking for a way out. Anna Tara was the only other person on stage, and she held out her hands in a posture of surrender. Unsure of what to do next, Tatiana dropped the knife and ran toward the wings. Before she disappeared behind the curtains, she glanced over her shoulder where she'd seen her father. He was gone.

Two men in suits collapsed on her, wrapping her up and taking her into custody.

"What are you doing to me?" Tatiana said. "I didn't do anything."

"Because all ballet dancers flit around carrying knives?" one of the men said sarcastically. "Please, spare me the innocence act."

"You're in big trouble, little lady," the other guard said.

As Tatiana eavesdropped on the conversations of the men surrounding her, they seemed to be just as confused as she was as to the whereabouts of President Michaels and President Petrenko. After a few minutes, one of the men ushered her into a dark SUV. Following a short drive across the city, she found herself inside a small interrogation room in the FBI's downtown offices.

Tatiana sat alone in the room, hands restrained and attached to the table in front of her, a blanket over her shoulders. A single tear inched down her cheek. She could feel her makeup running too.

More than an hour passed before a woman sauntered into the room and slid her notepad on the desk. She slumped into the chair across from Tatiana and leaned forward. Her hair was pulled taut in a bun. Snatching a pencil from behind her ear, she tapped the eraser onto the paper to an uptempo beat.

"I would ask you your name, but I doubt I'm going to get your real name," the woman said. "But my name is Alexis."

"My name is Emily."

She closed her eyes and slowly shook her head. "Did you really think I was going to fall for that?"

"That's my name."

"No, that's what your Russian handlers trained you to say, but we know that's not really the case now is it, Tatiana?"

She remained stoic despite the revelation that Alexis knew who she was. It was entirely possible that the Americans only knew her name and nothing else. That's why the general warned her that if she was captured, the Americans could learn her identity. But he said there was no guarantee that they knew who she really was or what she was up to.

"Never drop your cover," the general had told her. "Don't do the easy work for them. If they're going to break you, make them earn it. Otherwise, you're just giving up. Never give up."

Tatiana's lips quivered as more tears streamed down her face. "My name is Emily Smolov, and my father is a diplomat here. Perhaps you've heard of him? Yuri Smolov?"

"That's interesting," Alexis said. "Because I've read Mr. Smolov's file, and he doesn't have any children that I'm aware of."

"Maybe you don't know Mr. Smolov as well as you think you do."

Alexis shot her a sideways glance before pulling out her phone and typing on it.

"Might I suggest the search term 'Emily Smolov Yuri Smolov?'"

She glared at Tatiana. "Might I suggest you keep your mouth shut?"

After a few seconds, she stared, mouth agape at

the images on her phone.

"Did you find them?" Tatiana asked, half hoping, half asking.

Alexis turned her phone around and held out the screen so Tatiana could see it.

"There we are," she said, her expression unmoved by the picture that affirmed her story was true. "I told you. However, I also don't need to tell you about the diplomatic immunity I receive as a household member of the Russian delegation."

"I wasn't aware that Mr. Smolov had any children your age," Alexis said. "This comes as a big surprise to me, though I'm not about to let a couple of pictures on the Internet settle the issue for me."

She swallowed hard, trying not to cry anymore, trying to make the general proud. Though it wasn't easy. Tatiana wanted to sob buckets and then strangle someone. But none of that would help her cause at the moment.

Stick to your cover, Tatiana.

Alexis slid the document aside and clasped her hands together, interlocking her fingers. Leaning nearly halfway across the table, her eyes met Tatiana's gaze.

"I don't care who your *papa* is; you can't get away with everything here," she said.

"Then please tell me what I did. I don't

remember trying to kill anyone."

"I'm no stooge, *Emily*. I know who you are and what you were doing up on stage, even if you didn't actually do anything. Now, we don't have any record of your entrance into this country, so it would be in your best interest to tell us the truth, starting right now."

"Why don't you ask my father?" she said. "He will tell you whatever you need to know."

"Well, I would, except he's not available at the moment," Alexis said. "Apparently, your father was at the Kennedy Center tonight. What a strange coincidence that he was there too and you just so happened to be standing on stage armed with a knife when the dance ended."

"He's been arrested?" Tatiana asked.

"You could say that," Alexis said as she eased another picture out of the folder. Tatiana stared at the image, gently stroking her dad's face in the photograph.

"Now, are you going to tell me what I need to know? Or do I have to use far more painful means to get you to comply? The choice is yours."

Tatiana crossed her arms and stared out the window at a mixture of faint stars and Washington's lights winking back at her.

"I already told you the truth," she said. "The choice

is yours of whether you want to believe me or some story you've already made up in your head about me."

Alexis sighed as she stood. "Fine. Have it your way. I can promise you that you won't like what's about to happen next."

She exited the room, closing the door behind her. When it latched shut, Tatiana sobbed and heaved over what she'd just endured. Keeping a straight face after seeing the photograph of Yuri Smolov was one of the hardest things she'd ever done.

The general had always told her to stick to the cover and everything would be all right, so she did, trusting his advice without question. And he delivered, though she wasn't sure what the FBI agent was going to see when he searched for her alias along with that of a Russian spy masquerading as a diplomat.

And never did she once think that it would be an actual picture, one she'd often seen the first thing when she awoke each morning and the last thing she saw before she went to bed.

After seeing her father at The Kennedy Center, Tatiana started to wonder if he was going to be the one to extract her. And if he was, perhaps he was working with the Russian government in a special capacity.

But until she laid eyes on that photo, she'd never once considered that her father was indeed a spy.

CHAPTER 39

A HOOD DROPPED OVER BLACK's head before he was led out of the underground entrance in handcuffs. While he had no idea where he was ultimately going, he could hear the men speaking in hushed tones and knew it wouldn't be good. He wanted to hear Shields's voice come through clear in his ear piece, but she wasn't saying a word. Not that it mattered. Black's coms had been discovered and destroyed right in front of him, stomped on by one of the arresting FBI agents.

"The fun is just beginning," one of the men next to Black said.

A door opened and then shut. Black sensed there was at least one other person in the car.

"Bet you didn't expect your night to go like this, did you?" Black said.

There was a moment of silence before he heard a response.

"I'm guessing that makes two of us," a man replied.

Black scooted back in his seat. "I didn't do what they're accusing me of, you know."

"I'm not the judge, just the executioner. Someone else makes those decisions, not me. I just follow orders."

"You don't always have to follow orders."

"You see, that's where you're wrong," the man said. "If I don't follow orders, things don't go well for me. And that's the difference between me and you. When you do what you're told, things can go very badly."

"So, what are you going to do? Shoot me in the back of the head and bury me in a shallow grave?"

The man huffed through his nose. "No, it'll be very deep. Nobody is ever going to find your body. I'll make sure of that much."

"Are you gonna take this hood off or at least be man enough to look me in the eyes?"

"Me doing my job isn't a test of my masculinity nor is it wise for you to challenge me that way. I might shoot you right now."

There was the sound of someone tapping on the window followed by a hum as it rolled down.

"I need you to do something else tonight," said another man from outside.

The alarm chimed, warning that the door was open on the idling vehicle. The other voice sounded familiar, but Black couldn't quite place it. He was sure someone else was now sitting in the driver's seat. The clicking of the car being placed in gear was followed by the roar of the engine as Black lurched forward.

"Where are we going?" Black asked.

"As far away from here as we can get without anyone tailing us," the man said.

"Don't I know you?" Black asked. "Who are you?"

The driver chuckled. "We've met on several occasions before. And I apologize for the rude manner in which you were treated. I would've removed the hood, but I didn't have time. If I didn't get you out of there any sooner, there's no telling what would've happened to you, especially with that hothead agent itching to put a bullet in your head."

"I'm sorry, but I didn't catch your name," Black said, leaning forward.

"Of course you didn't because I didn't say it. And it might be best that you don't know."

"What are you going to do with me?"

"I'm going to make sure you're dead."

* * *

A HALF-HOUR later, the vehicle came to a stop. Black listened as the engine powered down and the man doing the driving was now checking his weapon.

"I suggest you take it nice and easy," the man said

as he grabbed Black and led him outside. They walked away from the vehicle for about a minute in what sounded like a forest.

He had heard the man's voice before but couldn't place it. While the idea of getting mysteriously murdered in the woods wasn't exactly how Black expected to die, he at least wanted to know who was about to end his life.

"Can you at least let me see your face before you shoot me?"

The man chuckled. "Who said anything about shooting you?"

"I don't know if this is some kind of game to you or not, but I—"

Black froze as his hood was ripped off and he came face to face with his chauffeur—and his executioner—for the past thirty minutes.

"You look kinda surprised, kid," the man said.

Black's jaw fell agape. "Robert Besserman?"

"In the flesh."

"But I thought—"

"Just calm down," Besserman said in not much more than a whisper. "This is all for show. There's a camera running on us and has been ever since I got into the car. It won't be able to capture our voices from this distance if we speak softly, so I'm only going to tell you this once. You need to kneel facing this grave here on the left. When I shoot you in the back of the head with my paintball gun, I'm going to fire my real weapon. The camera will hear that. You fall forward into the pit. I'll shovel dirt onto the one on the right, and nobody will be the wiser. Everyone will think you're dead. We'll report it in the papers, and that'll be the end of that."

"Is my career as an operative about to end?"

"Hardly," Besserman said. "In fact, you're just getting started. You won't believe the kind of missions you'll be able to take on now that you're about to be dead."

"And the rest of the team?"

"They'll be the only ones aside from me who know what's really about to happen."

"Well, let's get this over with then," Black said.

"One more thing," Besserman said. "There's a cell phone and a flashlight in the hole in front of you. After you hear me drive off, call Shields on the number programmed in the address book. She'll come get you about a quarter-mile from here by the main road. And good luck."

Besserman shouted at Black to assume the position. He knelt in front of the grave and took a deep breath.

The red bead from the paintball gun splattered against Black's head as he heard the shot from the real gun. He tumbled forward into the grave and lay there for what felt like an hour before Besserman finished filling the grave. After he drove off, Black followed the instructions he was given and then smiled wryly as he lumbered down the dirt road toward civilization.

His death was a rebirth of sorts, giving him a chance to re-invent himself.

Nobody will ever see me coming.

CHAPTER 40

One week later

BLACK SMOOTHED OUT THE EDGES of his costume mustache and finger combed the wispy hair from his wig over to the right. The windy conditions at Virginia Beach meant that he would be in a constant tug of war between the breeze and wishing to appear like he wasn't entirely ancient. He looked at his outfit in the rearview mirror one last time before climbing out of his car and trudging through the sand.

When he reached the boardwalk, which served as the *de facto* entrance to the beach, Black stopped to talk to an old man chewing on a cigar and struggling with a pair of chairs.

"Does your back really hurt you that much?" Black asked the elderly man.

The man glared at Black. "You think you're cute, don't you? Some whippersnapper cruising around like you're always going to be that way. Well, I got news for you, sonny. Your body is going to break down one day just like everybody else's."

"But I already look like I'm five hundred years old."

The old man dropped his chair and stood upright. "I would've made you look older if you didn't act so damned sprightly all the time."

It was Blunt, whose disguise wasn't nearly as impressive as Black's.

"Thanks for letting me do this," Black said.

"If I hadn't agreed to it, you would've persisted until I either punched your lights out or let you."

Black's eyebrows shot upward as he grinned. "You would've punched my lights out?"

"Back in the day, I would have."

"I'm glad you've mellowed, for your sake."

Blunt took the cigar out of his mouth and eyed Black closely. "There's a reason you're on this team. And I think that attitude of yours right there sums it up. I don't want anybody around me who's satisfied with being second best."

"If you're not winning, what's the point?"

Blunt nodded. "I still would've kicked your ass back in the day. Now get down to the water. She's waiting for you. She just wanted five more minutes."

Black strode across the sand in the late September sun. Most beachgoers were packing up to head back home. But not Tatiana.

She was fifteen years old but looked like a six-year-old planted in the sand and working on her masterpiece.

"Mind if I help you?" Black asked as he sat down next to her.

Tatiana shrugged. "It's a free country—at least that's what I hear."

Snatching a nearby empty bucket, Black filled it with sand and packed it down tight. "It's free, but it's not perfect, you know. We have our flaws like everyone else. Do you think your country is perfect?"

Tatiana shook her head subtly. "I don't know what to think any more. It's hard to put faith in anything when you find out that your entire life was a lie."

"I'm sure your father loved you," Black said.

"No, he didn't. He loved his job. He loved his country. But he simply tolerated us."

"Well, I know how you feel."

Tatiana looked up and glared at Black. "You know what it's like to have your father permit an intelligence agency to kidnap you at the age of thirteen and then train for two years to kill someone, only to have your entire world turned upside down at the exact moment you were supposed to do your job?"

"Not exactly."

"Then don't patronize me by telling me that you know how I feel."

Black turned the bucket over, emptying the cylindrical sand along the wall Tatiana had been building. "I lost my father in the most brutal of ways in Afghanistan. He parachuted out of a plane when it was struck by a Taliban missile. Even before his feet hit the ground, several dozen members of the Taliban didn't even bother to release him from his harness. They scooped up the chute and tied it to the back of a pickup truck, dragging him back and forth through the street until he died from the injuries. I never even got to see his broken and battered body again. I never got to tell him goodbye. I never got to tell him how much I loved him."

"Does it get any easier?" she asked.

He shook his head. "I miss him every day. It's why I keep his dog tags around my neck and close to my heart. I don't ever want to forget him."

"I spent most of my childhood longing for my father's attention despite how he treated me, but he was never around to give me what I really wanted," Tatiana said. "And I spent two years wondering if he'd appreciate me the way the general did if I succeeded in my mission. Then in a matter of minutes, I notice my father, who is telling me not to go through with it. I ignore him. The lights go out. And when the light returns, I'm left on stage with a knife in my hand and my father nowhere in sight."

"He's not coming back, Tatiana."

She nodded knowingly. "He's dead, isn't he?"

"I'm afraid so."

"Who killed him?" she asked.

"Will that change anything?"

Tatiana sighed. "No, but it might give me some more closure."

"The truth is it doesn't matter. Nothing will bring him home. Trust me. I know that from experience. No amount of revenge or retribution will raise a person from the dead. But there's still hope for you. There's still a chance that you can be resurrected, salvaged off life's trash heap. But it's up to you now. Today is a new chapter in your life. You don't have to spend it as a spy. You can be a normal kid, go to high school, then to college. Get a degree in a field where you can do something you love."

"Is that what you did?" she asked.

"I'm not exactly the best at taking my own advice." Black stood up and backed away from the sandcastle.

"Thanks for your help," she said.

"I barely did anything."

"You helped," she said as she stood and joined him. "And it's beautiful."

Black admired their work. "My stepdad hated sandcastles."

"My dad loved them," she said. "I'm ready to go."

Black walked her back to the SUV waiting in the parking lot. He opened the door for her and wished her good luck before closing it. He didn't move as the vehicle drove off.

"Nice 'stache," a woman said behind him.

Black spun around to see Shields. "What are *you* doing here?"

"Just wanted to see how you were doing."

"Senator Gaither is going to prison after the information dumped on the world by Wikileaks has undone him. That's a good thing. And I was exonerated for Captain Watkins murder and Gaither's attempted murder, posthumously, of course."

"Is being dead all it's cracked up to be?"

"Hardly, especially when you have to live through it. There are people out there who think I was killed by a Russian spy. That's almost as bad as if that actually did happen."

"I'm surprised you and that ego of yours can fit through the door sometimes."

"It's a burden," Black said. "But I'm willing to bear it."

Shields shook her head. "Seriously, how are you?"

"I'm always doing well when justice is being served."

"Our work will never be done, you know? There's always someone else out there concocting a scheme to hurt others for personal gain."

"Or for their country's gain."

"Speaking of which, Blunt has a new assignment for us."

"Already?"

She nodded. "I told him you'd be ready to go."

Black winked. "I'm always ready to go. I was just hoping to school you at the shooting range."

"In your dreams, spook," she said.

"So, what's the job?"

"Apparently, Gaither was just one cog in a much greater wheel."

"You mean there are more crooked politicians?" Black said. "Consider me shocked."

"I brought your gear," she said. "Wheels up in an hour."

"Roger that. Let's roll."

THE END

ACKNOWLEDGMENTS

I am grateful to so many people who have helped with the creation of this project and the entire Titus Black series.

Krystal Wade was a big help in editing this book as always.

I would also like to thank my advance reader team for all their input in improving this book along with all the other readers who have enthusiastically embraced the story of Titus Black. Stay tuned ... there's more Titus Black coming soon.

ABOUT THE AUTHOR

R.J. PATTERSON is an award-winning writer living in southeastern Idaho. He first began his illustrious writing career as a sports journalist, recording his exploits on the soccer fields in England as a young boy. Then when his father told him that people would pay him to watch sports if he would write about what he saw, he went all in. He landed his first writing job at age 15 as a sports writer for a daily newspaper in Orangeburg, S.C. He later attended earned a degree in newspaper journalism from the University of Georgia, where he took a job covering high school sports for the award-winning *Athens Banner-Herald* and *Daily News.*

He later became the sports editor of *The Valdosta Daily Times* before working in the magazine world as an editor and freelance journalist. He has won numerous writing awards, including a national award for his investigative reporting on a sordid tale surrounding an NCAA investigation over the University of Georgia football program.

R.J. enjoys the great outdoors of the Northwest while living there with his wife and four children. He still follows sports closely. He also loves connecting with readers and would love to hear from you. To stay updated about future projects, connect with him over Facebook or on the inter-webs at www.RJPbooks.com and sign up for his newsletter.